Slipstream

A Science Fiction continuance

TOM WILLISON

AuthorHouse™ LLC
1663 Liberty Drive
Bloomington, IN 47403
www.authorhouse.com
Phone: 1-800-839-8640

Published by AuthorHouse 07/18/2014

ISBN: 978-1-4969-2280-9 (sc)
ISBN: 978-1-4969-2279-3 (e)

Library of Congress Control Number: 2014911531

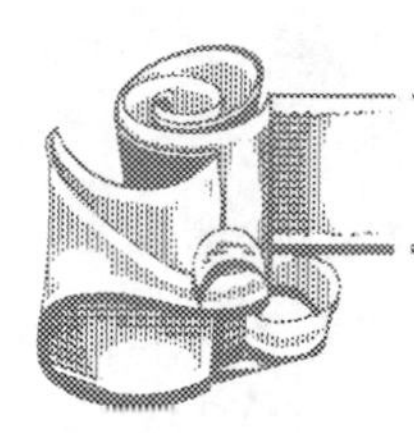

CHAPTER 1

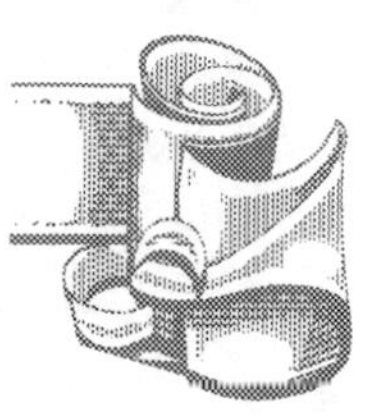

A black Honda Helix motor scooter traveled west on 62nd Street in northwest Indianapolis. It entered the rear parking lot of the abandoned office building once occupied by the defunct Pence Technology Corporation. It was past 10 p.m. and a small security light on the building glared down on the rider as he parked the bike and dismounted.The rider was dressed in black trousers topped with a black leather riding jacket. He removed his helmet and replaced it with a dark ski mask and crept toward the back wall of the building. From a satchel, he removed a grappling hook and unwound the rope. Whirling the hook, he tossed it up over the roof ledge of the building. It caught with a brisk pull of the rope and, with satchel over his shoulder, he scaled the wall of the building. He moved to the right side of the roof. Carefully chalking out a five foot by five foot square, he removed a hand-held industrial laser from the satchel and began cutting through the first layer of the roof covering. Then came the overlay board, the insulation, the structural joist, the vapor control layer, the roof decking and finally, the ceiling. Each layer was put aside on the roof or dropped to the floor within. The rider then looked down into the interior of the building. So far, so good.

Moving the grappling hook to the opposite side of the ledge, he dropped the rope down through the roof opening and scaled down to the floor below. Before him was the ACC Main Frame Computer, left behind when the building was abandoned. It was the one remaining of three main frame computers owned and operated by Gerald Pence, CEO of the recently shuttered Pence Technology Corporation.

The rider pulled a cell phone from his pocket and buttoned on.

"All set. Move in."

Almost instantly, the sound of a helicopter broke the still of the night. It approached the building, hovered over the roof and lowered a sling through the opening to the waiting man below.

The sling was secured to the main frame and lifted up through the hole.

"Take off. I'll join you in about two hours." messaged the dark stranger.

The helicopter turned north and faded into the night with its cargo swaying on the tether below.

Steve Gordon and Becky sat quietly on the back deck of their house and gazed into the September evening sky. It was a clear, warm night, and the stars...away from the lights of the town of Williams Creek... shone brightly.

A meteor flashed across the sky and then gave way to earth's atmosphere.

"Make a wish,"Becky whispered.

"A wish? All my wishes have been answered." Steve chuckled.

A sweep of breeze rustled the leaves on the trees below the deck and a hoot owl let it be known of his presence some distance off. Both Steve and Becky sat silently digesting the calmness of the setting.

Becky glanced up at Steve and then away. What was he thinking about, she thought...Carolyn...his deceased wife? He was.

Steve's eyes searched the starry sky deep in thought. Carolyn, his wife of twenty-four years had died of cancer in September of last year. For his two sons and Steve, it had been the most trying time of their lives.

The loneliness that was thrust upon Steve, the despair and concern for their father wrenching the minds of both Steven, Jr. and Robert, dug deeply into their lives. It was nights like this that stimulated this nostalgia and there was no way of disguising it.

Becky knew it. They were due to be married this month...next Sunday, September 20 to be exact. There had already been two postponements. Steve seemed uncertain about the commitment. After all, Carolyn had been gone for less than a year. Would it be proper?

Steve loved Becky. No question about it. But still, there was that lingering doubt.

Becky sensed all this and squeezed Steve's hand in understanding.Then Steve's mind went back to November of last year and the events involving Gerald Pence and his state-of-the-art aircraft....the Altair. It was all so obscure.

The parlor of the farm house was full of expectant people as Gerald Pence entered.

"Everyone have a seat."

Steve, Steven, Jr., Robert, Janet....Gerald's ex-secretary and now lover, his daughter, Becky, and Homer and Anna.... Gerald's farm house guardians,...all obeyed.

"I've got quite a bit to say. It's my feeling that the FBI is hot on my trail and it would behoove me to move quickly. You've probably noticed all the cars leaving the farm. All but the essential people have vacated the lab, so after a few minor details, I'll be ready to take off in the Altair."

"But I thought ..." Becky stuttered.

"You thought it was happening tonight. Well, things have changed. Steve, I want you to leave with your group right away. I want you to take Becky and Janet with you"

Janet bolted up in her chair. "No, Gerald, I'm not leaving you! Whatever you do or wherever you go, I want to be with you!"

"Janet, I can't let you be a part of this!"

"Gerald, please"

Gerald walked over to the fireplace and placed his hands on the mantle. He was momentarily deep in thought. He turned to the group.

"Folks, here are the facts of life. I am now a fugitive from the United States government. I've broken the law and I've developed something that the authorities would go to any extreme to get hold of. I've already told you how I regret that! I've got to go where no one can find me or the Altair!"

"Where would that be?" Robert and Steven Jr. inquired almost simultaneously.

"You don't need to know that. Just do as I ask."

"I will not leave you!" Janet shouted.

Gerald gave her a hard stare, but said nothing.

"What 'bout the property?" Homer asked.

"It won't be livable here soon. I suggest that you and Anna go back to your home in Elkhart. Your jobs are done."

"Does that go for me?" Tears rolled down Janet's cheeks as she asked.

"Janet, dear, I don't want to take the chance that this whole thing may literally blow up! Please understand. I love you. That's why I want you to go with Steve."

"I love you, and that's why I'm not leaving!" Janet screamed.

Gerald shrugged in resignation. He looked over to the rest of the group and rolled his eyes.

"I could bind and gag her, but heaven help me if I tried."

"Dad, can't you tell us what you have in mind?" Becky asked.

*"No, I can't, Honey. Just go with Steve. Judging from what I've seen, you deserve to have the kind of future you'll have with him. Now..before it's too late... everyone! Haul ass!*Becky shook Steve out of his thoughts.

"Another shooting star!"

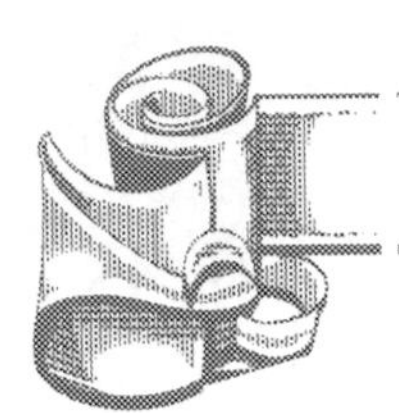

CHAPTER 2

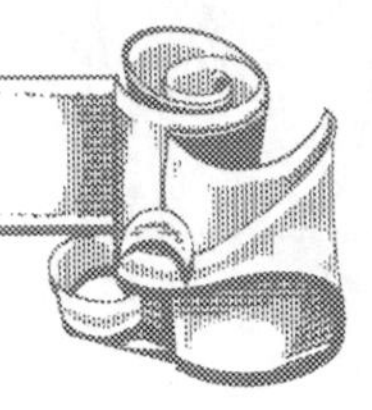

Doc Ewing, Labor Supervisor of Williams Creek State Park and Steve Gordon's immediate boss, was distraught when he read the telegram. Marine Staff Sergeant Jon Ewing, his son, had been seriously wounded during a skirmish in Afghanistan and had been flown to a hospital in Frankfurt, Germany, in critical condition. Still in a state of shock, he cell-phoned Steve at the Nature Center. He explained his situation and relayed his plans fly to Frankfurt.

"While I'm gone, I want you to take over for me." he told Steve without expecting what followed.

"You go ahead, Doc. Becky and I can postpone our wedding until you get back."

"Postpone?" Doc answered highly irritated. "Good God, Steve, you've already done that twice. Becky won't buy it! Go ahead with the wedding and save me the guilt trip!"

"Becky deserves a nice honeymoon," Steve retorted," and we can't do that while I've got this responsibility."

There was pause on Doc's end..

"Steve, I've got to be with Jon. For all I know, he might not be alive by the time I get there, but I've got to go. I'm not going to feel bad about this, because, quite frankly, mister, I think you're using it as another excuse to salve some sort of silly notion about remarrying!"

Now there was silence on Steve's end. He calmly responded.

"Please let me deal with this on my own terms, Doc. You go....I'll take care of things here."

"I'm catching a military transport out of Indianapolis tonight, Steve. You do what you think you have to, but please think about Becky in all this." He switched off.

Steve placed the cell phone on his desk and sat silently staring at it. Yes....think about Becky in all this, he thought.

The An-12 military transport took off from the Indianapolis International Airport that night, bound for Frankfurt, Germany. Doc Ewing was aboard. He sat on the port side by a window overlooking the diminishing landscape as the craft roared skyward toward its twenty thousand foot altitude.

It leveled off and maintained a steady, uneventful drone. He was slightly over nine hours away from his son's bedside.

The darkness of the night obliterated the ground below and Doc, bored with the view, settled back and reflected on the life of himself and his son, Jon.

It was 1977 when he met and married Nancy Gregory. He had graduated from Purdue two years earlier with a degree in Natural Resources and Environmental Science and was hired by The Indiana Department of Natural

Resources immediately thereafter. Nancy had become pregnant in early 1978, and had Jon that Fall. Three more pregnancies followed, each resulting in miscarriages which opened the door to her poor health and eventual death from breast cancer. Jon was ten then, and both he and Doc had taken the loss extremely hard.

The thought shook Doc back to the present and the drone of the An-12. He reviewed his conversation with Steve earlier in the day. Yes, he could understand Steve's reluctance to jump into another marriage after losing his wife to the same affliction. However, there had been a difference. Doc had never met another woman that he felt that he could truly love as much as he did Nancy. Thus, fourteen years went by with both him and the now twenty-four year old Jon in perpetual mourning.

Perhaps he and Steve had been unrealistic in different ways. Becky, Steve's bride to be, was a wonderful woman... just right to heal the loss of his first wife. His sons, Steven, Jr. and Robert, adored her and were more than willing to accept her as their new mother. Steve and his stupid morals, thought Doc.

.....And the drone went on.

Steve came home from the park early that evening, but did not discuss his conversation with Doc. He needed time to sort things out. He was rescued by the buzz of his cell phone. It was Robert.

"Hi, Pop! How are things in the boondocks?"

"Probably the same as they are up there. It's raining here. What about you?"

"Yeah, rain here too. Listen, I need to discuss something with you."

"Go ahead."

"Just before it all hit the fan, Mr. Pence gave his Iranian intern all his files on the plans and formulas for construction of the Altair. He was told to lock them up in our lab in the aeronautical building on campus."

"So?"

"This guy has spent weeks studying these files and I think he's planning on building his own version of the aircraft!"

"What makes you think that?"

Robert's voice intensified

"Dad, this guy has recruited a bunch of guys in our class to help him, including me. He's rented an abandoned hanger at the Purdue airport, and when he's not going to class, he spends most of his time there."

"You say you're part of the group...what goes on in this hanger?"

"Hell, I don't know, I've haven't gone out there yet."

"Do you think this kid has the wherewithal to actually duplicate the Altair?"

"Beats me, but the guy's a genius. If anyone can do it, he can. I think that's why Mr. Pence gave him the files."

"Robert, you heard Gerald Pence decry the fact that he built the Altair in the first place. Why would he encourage someone else to build one?"

There was silence on Robert's end.

"I don't know, but I thought you could give me some input."

"I would suggest you dump this whole thing and get back to your studies.....and stay away from this kid!"

Robert audibly smirked.

"That might be a problem, Dad. He's my roommate!"

Steve sat down at the dinner table across from Becky. He really wasn't hungry and he was noticeably preoccupied.

"What was that all about with Robert?" she asked.

Steve snickered, "He thinks his roommate is going to build another Altair."

"The Iranian boy?"

"I think that's what he said." Steve pushed his food around on the plate absently.

"He's a bright boy, but I don't think he can put together everything he'll need to do it." Becky said, smiled and then took a bite of food. She stared at Steve intently for moments as she chewed. There was an awkward silence, then Becky spoke up,

"Steve, what's bothering you? You can't be taking Robert's story that seriously."

Steve toyed with the food in front of him and finally put his fork down.

"I learned today that Doc's son, Jon, was seriously wounded over in Afghanistan. He's in a hospital in Germany and Doc's on his way over there." More silence.

"I'm terribly sorry to hear that. Who's managing things while he's gone?" She knew the answer before she asked. A bite of salad delayed Steve's response.

"I guess I am." He mumbled.

Becky put her fork in her plate and folded her hands under her chin and studied the man across from her. There was a long silence...too long for Steve.

"Where does that put our wedding?" she asked almost in a whisper.

"I reminded Doc of our wedding next Sunday and ....." Steve stuttered.

"He saw no problem with it, did he, Steve?" She finished.

"Honey, I think it's important for us to go on a honeymoon. We can't do that until Doc gets back and we can have our wedding and the honeymoon. You understand, don't you?"

"I understand that the wedding is off again! Yes, I understand, Steve."

Becky cleared the table, washed the dishes and went to bed.

Steve sat at the empty table until there was no longer any stirring in the house. He then went out onto the patio deck and stood in the rain until he was soaked to the skin.

The An-12 landed in Frankfurt on schedule. Doc called the US Military Headquarters there and received clearance to visit his son at the Frankfurt Hospital.

He walked down the hall of the hospital toward his son's room side by side with an American doctor.

"Tell me like it is." Doc asked nervously.

"Apparently, he was hit by a mortar shell which took out part of his lower extremities. He's lost a kidney, his left leg up to the knee, and part of his lower spine is severely damaged."

The Doctor put his hand reassuringly on Doc's shoulder as they entered Jon's room.

"But, he will survive, sir. It will be a long road back, but he will make it."

Doc could not restrain the tears.

"Thank you, Doctor."

He stood over his son's sleeping form and cried.

Robert decided go to the hanger at the Purdue Airport with his Iranian roommate, Farid Sherazi. What he saw amazed and frightened him.

Held in a rack,vertically, was the framework of what appeared to be the fuselage of a large disk. A visual sweep of the area revealed work benches and mechanical and electronic equipment, almost a duplicate of Pence's laboratory.

In a far corner of the hanger was a computer mainframe wired to several large illuminated computer screens.

Robert recognized several of his Raisbeck Engineering friends.

"What's going on here?" he asked one of them.

"Oh, Mister Genius over there", pointing toward Farid, "thinks he can reconstruct Mr. Pence's aircraft. I think the guy's nuts, but as long as we get some engineering credits, why not humor him?"

Robert motioned toward an elderly man standing with Farid.

"Who's he?"

The student replied with a smirk,

"You've got to meet Farid's father fresh out of the peaceful nation of Iran. Make sure Farid's around to interpret. The guy apparently has trouble with English."

"What the hell part does he play in all this?" Robert blurted.

The student started back to his work.

"Ask Farid," were his parting words.

Robert left the hanger without any further words with Farid, knowing he would talk to him later in the privacy of their room in the dorm. It was bad enough that his roommate had gone as far as he had in his ridiculous idea of rebuilding a version of the Altair, but why was his Iranian father involved in the project, he asked himself. This was all very mysterious.

Robert could not concentrate on his studies and finally went to bed at 2:20 in the morning. This was not the first time that Farid had not spent the night at the dorm.

There were many questions to be answered and before Robert finally fell asleep, he made up his mind to take his father's advice and drop out of any connection with this insane project.

Steve decided to stay at the nature center rather than the management office. He had a lot on his mind, and at the center he could relax and think.

The rain was still falling that morning which reduced the number of park tourists to almost zero. He spent a half hour feeding the creatures in the main exhibit area, then retired to the aviary room where he sat watching the birds from the one way window. The feeders had been replenished the day before and attracted the indigenous birds in large numbers. It normally was soothing to Steve, but now it brought back thoughts of the past.

When the two boys were young, he had built a bird sanctuary at their home similar to the one at the nature center, complete with the indoor-outdoor speaker system. The boys had become kings of the hill with their friends in the community as a result. But all that brought back memories of Carolyn.

Steve's first year at Depauw had taken him closer to his master's degree in Resource Management. In his second year, he became interested enough in the arts that he took time to visit Depauw's Peeler Art Center on a regular basis. That is where he met Carolyn.

On one visit in the Spring of 1976, he saw a very attractive girl busily engaged in sketching a version of a Renoir painting. He was more interested in the artist than in the art.

"I wish I had that talent." he quipped looking over her shoulder. Carolyn kept sketching without looking up.

"Most people can do more than they think they can." she said.

He replied," I can't draw a straight line."

"Your signature is a form of art. So, if you've ever written a check, you're an artist" Then she looked up. It was love at first sight for the both of them

They began dating off and on. She was also dating another man off campus, who was nine years her senior and the assistant pastor of the First Baptist Church in Greencastle..

As the year went on at the university, he found it more difficult to concentrate on his studies and compete with a man of God for the woman he loved. He had to resolve the issue.

They sat across from each other in the Hub diner inside the Memorial Student Union Building.

"I'm one year away from my masters degree. I might wind up in a very boring career. There's not a whole lot of exotic places to visit on business trips in the resource management business." Steve said as he sipped his coffee, "so you might be very unhappy married to a naturalist."

Carolyn choked on her Pepsi.

"Married!" she cleared her throat,"don't you know of my relationship with David?"

"The holy guy? Hell, you can't love him. Think how really bored you'd be catering to a bunch of church fogies for the rest of your life."

Carolyn laughed.

"When I was a little impressionable girl, I dreamt one day of my knight in shining armor proposing to me on bended knee."

Steve suddenly slid across his seat and dropped to one knee to the amusement of the other students in the diner.

"My armor is at the dry-cleaners, but will you marry me, my pretty Duicinea", he begged.

Carolyn buried her head in her arms on the table top and laughed uncontrollably. She raised her head in an effort to gather herself and guffawed again at the sight of Steve on his knee.

"You are a crazy man!" she giggled.

"Well...? I can't stay down here forever!"

She laughed again and finally wiped happy tears from her eyes.

"I guess Reverend David will have to handle all the fogies. Of course I will, you nut!"

The other students clapped and cheered.

A Pileated Woodpecker drummed a tree not far from the observation window and echoed into the woods surrounding the nature center, jolting Steve from his reveries.

The entrance bell jingled in the exhibit area and three tourists entered. Steve greeted them with mock cheerfulness, and asked if he could answer any questions. They responded with a "no thank you"and proceeded to browse the display and creature area, while Steve retired to his office in the rear of the building. Some people will tour an area, rain or shine, he thought with a smile.The guests migrated to the aviary room, and sat for some time observing and listening to the fluttering birds on the outside. They then thanked Steve and departed.

Steve left his office and strolled back to his bird watch. The pileated woodpecker had left the tree and was now banging loudly on the rain spout of the building.

That's it, Steve thought, call for your mate. Did I make that much fuss with Carolyn?

A trip to Linton, Indiana, Carolyn's home town, to meet her parents, and a grateful nod of approval opened the door for their wedding plans.

He had graduated in the spring of 1978, was immediately offered and accepted a position as Interpretive Naturalist at The Williams Creek State Park. Carolyn and Steve were married on September 20 of that year and moved into a cottage conveniently located close to the park.

The relationship was a happy one. They made each other laugh. Oh, there was occasional bickering like most couples, but more times than not, it ended in a laugh and a kiss.

Steven, Jr. was born on June 8th, 1980. The delivery was uneventful and Carolyn took it well. Then a year later, Robert came along. This time there was some problems with the delivery which occasioned a caesarean section. Both Carolyn and Robert survived in good order, but the experience led to the decision to call it a family.

It was to be a uniquely happy and laughing time through the twenty-three years of marriage until in the fall of 2000, they discovered a lump in Carolyn's left breast. Nothing serious the doctor had said. They would take care of it after the holidays.

The rain stopped late that afternoon. Too late to allow any further tourist traffic for the day, so Steve went home.

He came down the hallway to the kitchen where he found a note leaning against the napkin container on the table. He picked it up and read:

My dearest,

It has occurred to me that grieving over the loss of a loved one takes more time than we have allowed. I think the fact that you need that time to recover from your tragic loss makes it necessary for me to step aside. I'm staying with a close friend in Indianapolis. I will contact you if and when, in my opinion, the time has come for our relationship to resume in earnest.

My love forever,
Becky

Steve laid the note on the table. It was something he had expected but it still came as a shock.

The rumble of thunder and a torrent of fresh rain accentuated his mood. Once again, he stepped out onto the patio deck to receive the deluge, and walked to the rail.

"Carolyn... my God, why don't you go! Please, please leave me alone!" he screamed as a bolt of lightening revealed his tears among the falling rain against his face.

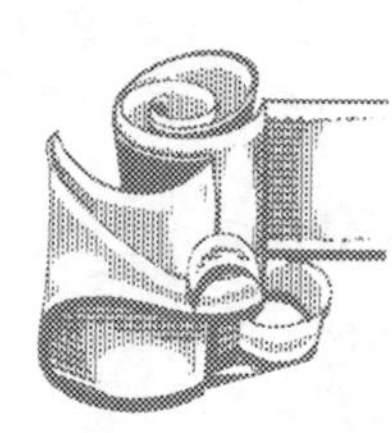

CHAPTER 3

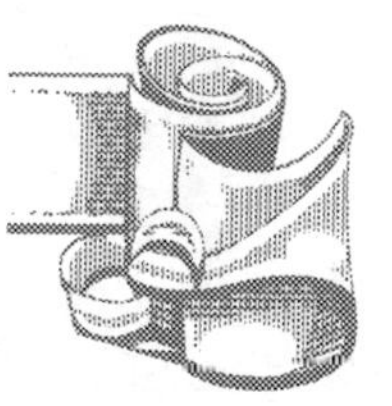

It was at the Goethe Link Observatory near Brooklyn, Indiana that several Indiana University students and their professor first noticed it. In the basement of the observatory, on a large computer screen, there were unidentified disturbances emanating from the direction that their radio and telescopes were pointed. Professor Grant Emerson of IU's Astronomy Department was at the computer as the signals were coming in. A group of six students stood behind him as he attempted to fine tune the phenomena.

"Ladies and gentlemen, these signals appear to be coming from the planet Mars, but I presently can't seem to make them out."

"Could they be coming from one of the rovers that NASA has sent up?" questioned one of the students.

"It could well be, but why has it not occurred before this?" Emerson responded. He turned to one of the students," Go topside and readjust the equipment. Perhaps we can get a better image."

That done, there appeared a discernible passage on the computer screen.

Mars
02/07/'03

"I left earth in my experimental craft, the Altair, last November with the idea of testing the craft's space capabilities. I was able to reach the moon in two days...better than Apollo's time. But then a strange thing happened. As we orbited to the back of the moon, we apparently slipped into a stream of dark energy which propelled us forward at incredible speed. The onboard computer was unable to cope with all this and we lost total control. In fact, I thought at the time we had entered the so called worm hole. Before we knew what had happened, the stream threw us out over the planet Mars...."

The reception began to breakup again, and Professor Emerson frantically spun dials in an attempt to re-establish it, to no avail. The computer screen sputtered blankly.

"This must be the doings of a crackpot or something. It couldn't be possible." The professor maintained.

Several calls to observatories in the area established that the contact appeared to be authentic. Observatories across the country, including the Mauna Kea Observatory in Hawaii, confirmed the contact.

"Who is this Gerald Pence?", the professor asked over his shoulder. A student spoke up.

"I've heard of Steve Gordon talk about him often."

"The Steve Gordon in our astronomy club?" Emerson inquired.

"Yes, his brother was involved in a project at Purdue that this guy Pence was behind. It had to do with this aircraft he is referring to in his messages. Apparently, whatever it was, worked."

The phone rang on the computer desk. The professor answered.

"This is Doctor Agatha Dunbar from The Steward Observatory at the University of Arizona. Is Professor Grant Emerson there?"

"Speaking" He responded.

"We are confirming this contact from Mars"

"Unfortunately, we have lost the transmissions." the professor informed the caller.

"Our equipment is more sophisticated than yours. We're still receiving his signals. We'll up load them to you."

"It might be of interest to your group that one of our students' father was involved in the aircraft project."

"That is interesting," Dunbar responded," That would explain his last transmission that asked about his daughter, who is apparently the fiancé of your student's father."

"I will wait for your uploads, and in the meantime will try to get more information from this student of ours." They hung up.

A student was assigned to contact Steven, Jr. at the university that evening, and in the mean time the professor returned to the computer screen. The Arizona upload came through.

Mars
02/07/'03

"We entered the Mars atmosphere and landed in the northern region about 30 kilometers from the ice cap.Yes, Mars is red and very dusty. Our main computer was temporarily out of commission and our back-ups took over. Under my orders to the computer, we began roaming the area. It is as desolate as NASA"s rovers indicate. the Altair protects us from the high carbon atmosphere and the ultra-violet sun rays, which allows us to roam the area with impunity. Our first line computer was restored late in the Martian afternoon, which gave us much more flexibility.

The wind is very high here, so the dustthat was constantly being blown up severely restricts our vision. As the day dwindled, it grew very cold, but again our craft protected us from the freezing temperature.As the twilight set in, we discovered what appeared to be a cave close by. We ventured toward it and ultimately entered it. A very large, deep cavern. Its very warm temperature registered with the Altair computer and indicated that there was enough oxygen in the atmosphere that we could leave our craft with minimum protective clothing and masks. This we did, although my companion was very reluctant and very frightened. I became curious about the depth of the cave and the fact that the backend was a rocky descent. I sent Janet back to the ship while I ventured deeper into the cave. As I lowered myself over the boulders, a liquid sound greeted me. Unless my imagination was playing tricks on me, there might be water on Mars, very close to the surface."

The phone rang and Professor Emerson answered.

"This is Steven Gordon, sir. I understand you wanted to talk to me."

The professor put the computer on hold.

"This is much too bizarre to explain over the phone. Where are you? I will send one of the students to bring you here."

"What's this about, Professor?"

"You wouldn't believe me if told you!"

It had been three days since Doc Ewing arrived in Frankfurt to be with his son, Jon. Well aware of the damage done to him caused by a shell burst during his deployment in Afghanistan, Jon's battle with depression was severe. Doc was trying as best he could to pull him out of it.

"Word is that you did pretty well over there. It was what you did that saved your whole platoon I'm told."

Jon covered his eyes with his arm as a tear trickled down his cheek. Doc stood up from his chair beside the bed and strolled to the window over looking the hospital courtyard.

"I'm told you have a couple of medals coming to you." Doc said realizing how trivial the comment was.

Jon was again not responsive. He turned away from Doc and feigned sleep.

Doc shook his head in resignation and walked from the room into the hallway.I wish there was something I could do to snap the kid out of it, he thought.

A young man on crutches came down the hall and approached him.

"Are you Mr. Ewing?" he asked.

"Yes."

"Do you mind if we sit down? I'm still not used to these things." the young man said, flaunting the crutches.

They moved to a bench further down the hall, and sat.

The boy laid his crutches down beside him and grinned.

"I used to think it would be fun to hop around on these things."

The young man broke the silence.

"You must be proud of your son."

"I've always been proud of Jon." Doc answered.

"I was with him when he got it, sir. In fact, it was the same blast that gave me this bum foot. I don't think I'd be here if it weren't for your son."

Doc turned toward the youngster with brightened interest.

"Tell me what happened!" Doc requested.

"Our platoon was on patrol in Afghanistan's Korengal Valley when the bad guys ambushed us. One of our guys was hit and Sergeant Ewing, in spite of enemy fire, pulled him back to cover. He later saved another guy, while trying to pull the platoon together. That's when the insurgents got hold of me and tried to take me prisoner. Your son went after them, killed two of them, and drove the others off. We both tried to duck back to the platoon, which by that time was under cover and returning fire. It was then that a mortar shell hit behind us and blasted us both. I was hurt, but the Sergeant was hurt worse and really bleeding around his legs. Ignoring his injuries, he dragged me up to the platoon line and safety. After our platoon drove the attackers away, we rushed your son to the medics. We knew he was hurt bad."

Doc's throat was dry when he spoke.

"Jon was always an impulsive kid. It sounds just like him," he forced a soft smile.

The young man continued.

"When we got back to the CP, we told the Company CO what had happened, and he was quite impressed. I think your son will surely get some kind of medal."

Doc was silent as he folded his hands between his knees and stared blankly at the floor.

"I'm sure he'd rather have his leg back." Silence again,

"What is your name?" Doc asked.

"Joe...Private first-class Joseph Braddock, sir. My great grandfather used to be the heavy weight boxing champion of the world."

Doc perked up.

"Jimmy Braddock, of course. One of the finest fighters of all time. You would have made him proud."

A nurse came up to Doc.

"Excuse me, sir, but your son is asking for you."

Doc shook hands with Private Braddock and bade him farewell.

"Come see my Jon soon. I'm sure he'd want to talk to you"They parted, and Doc went back to the room.

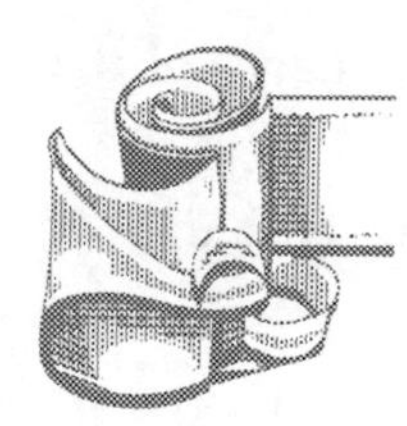

CHAPTER 4

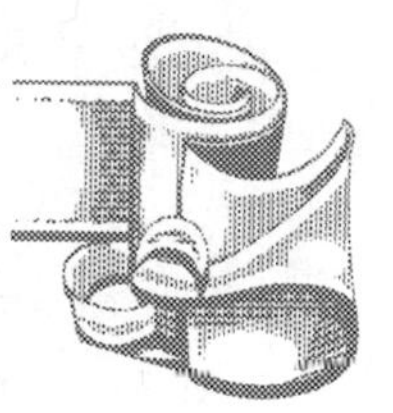

Farid's high tenor voice annoyed Robert immensely, but over a period of one semester at Purduc he got used to it. Lately, however, Farid had rarely spent time in their dorm room. Robert's brief trip to the hanger at the Purdue airport had revealed why. Farid was actually trying to duplicate the Altair from plans and formulas left to him by its creator, Gerald Pence.

It was one of those rare times Farid was in their dorm room when Robert returned from a late afternoon class. Much to Farid's discomfort, they sat down to talk.

"I am told you are very concerned about my uncle's presence at our airport project." Farid twanged.

"Uncle! They said he was your father!"

"Some sort of relative, I suppose. His name is Amir Jahangir, and he is a prominent engineer in Iran."

"Is he a citizen?" Robert asked.

"No, he's here on a B1 visas."

Robert became visibly disturbed.

"What business is he here for?"

"Aircraft construction." Farid responded and opened one of his text books indicating a desire to terminate the conversation. Robert planted a hand on the pages of the text book.

"Farid, I don't mean to upset you, but does that aircraft construction have to do with your project?'

"*Our* project! Aren't you part of it?" Farid asked pulling the text book away from Robert.

"No...not anymore. I've got my studies to worry about."

"You were part of Pence's venture. Why not this one?" Farid whined.

"I came aboard late in his program, so I didn't contribute much to it. Besides, the Altair, at that point, was pretty much a done deal, not someone's illusion!"

Farid slammed his textbook shut.

"You consider what I'm doing an illusion?"

Robert stood up and paced the room.

"Farid, be real! You might have the so called plans and formulas, but what else do you have?"

"I have all I need. I have a new formula for the composition of the aircraft skin. I have a new propulsion system....far superior to Pence's craft. I have Pence's mainframe computer that will program the terminals aboard the aircraft when we reach that stage."

"Pence's mainframe? Where the hell did you get that?" Robert demanded.

Farid reopened his textbook and smugly looked at Robert.

"Pence blew-up the mainframes in his home, and in his laboratory, but he forgot the one in his office. When his corporation folded, they closed up the office building so quickly, the computer was left behind."

Robert sat at the table again.

"How did you.....?" He started.

Farid finished the question, ... "Get it out of the building? Don't worry about that. I have my connections."

"Would that connection have anything to do with your uncle's involvement in this whole thing?"

Farid stood up and walked to the door.

"No comment. I'll be off to the airport." He left the room and the dormitory.

Robert sat for some time staring at the door and thinking. It was almost dark when he walked into the lobby of the dormitory and to the pay phone on the wall.

He fingered through the tattered phone book until he came to the page he was looking for. Placing a quarter in the coin slot he dialed a number. It rang three times.

"This is The Federal Bureau of Investigation, Special Agent Holtz speaking. How may I help you?"

A message came from NASA Headquarters, Washington, DC. to the Jet Propulsion Laboratory in California. A question was asked and answered:

"Mars is currently close to earth, so it might be possible to reach this guy through the radio frequency on his craft if we knew what it was. We'll try to trace it during his next transmission".

Mars

03/ 14/'03

"You won't believe this, but when I walked further down the back of the cave to trace the

sound of the liquid, I came upon a huge lake of either pure water or liquid carbon dioxide. There was no vapor visible so I assume that what I saw was pure water. It extended as far back as the darkness of the cave would allow me to see and glowed a green, sulfuric color at the bottom of the lake.There appears to be a strong sulfur presence on the planet.With my flashlight I noticed strange dark, elongated shapes along the side shores of the lake, but couldn't make out what they were. It wasn't until I saw one move that it occurred to me that I had found life on Mars."

At the Jet Propulsion Lab, "No luck with the frequency, but we'll keep trying."

Steven was disquieted,

"What do you mean she's gone?"

"Just what I said....she's gone." Steve answered.

"What's wrong, Dad? I don't like the tone of your voice."

"It's a long story, son, and I don't have time to explain it right now. I'll call you tonight when I get home from the park, and we'll talk."

There was a long pause.

"The wedding's off again, isn't it?"

"We'll talk tonight."

"That complicates things." Steven persisted

"What does that mean?" Steve asked with a noticeable pique.

"My story's long too, but I'll cut it short. We've been in touch with Gerald Pence."

"Good God, where is he?" Steve blurted.

"It's impossible to explain it over the phone, Dad. Please come to the Goethe Link Observatory tonight and we'll explain everything."

"Mysteries, eh?"

"Please, Dad."

"What does this all have to do with Becky?"

"Tonight!" Steven concluded and hung up.

Steve cradled the phone briskly.

He walked into the kitchen, poured himself a cup of coffee, and sat down at the table to think.

He had yet to locate Becky. She was with a friend in Indianapolis—but where in Indianapolis, and with what friend? Whenever Doc returned to the park, Steve could ferret all this out. If his relationship with Becky could be saved, the date of the wedding would be set, and under no circumstances would it be changed. This would be it. But what the hell is going on at the Goethe Link Observatory, and how does Becky fit into it all? Steve wondered.

It was time to leave for the park. He pulled on his jacket, and left the house. Moments later, the phone rang. After seven rings, the answering machine took the call.

"Steve, This is Becky. I won't bother you at work. I have some exciting news. I'll call tonight." The machine clicked off.

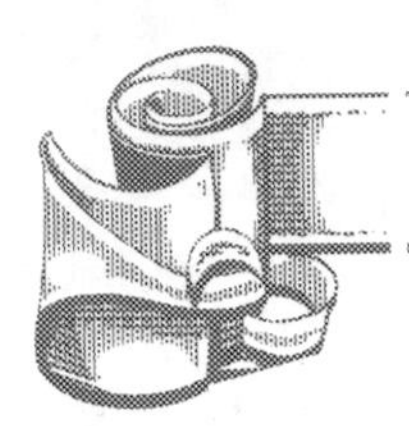

CHAPTER 5

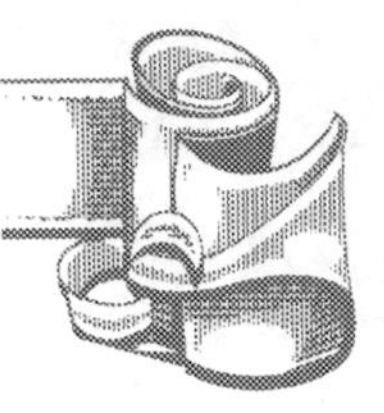

The sacral damage to Jon's spine was not as severe as it first appeared, and this phase of his rehabilitation went rapidly. Loss of one of his kidneys would not effect the body function of the other as long as it was healthy, which it was. Thus, Jon's recovery from his battle injuries were mainly his ability to psychologically cope with the loss of the lower part of his left leg. The wound at least was healing well, and the doctors were talking about an imminent return to the United States for extended rehab.

Nurse Crista Braun entered Jon's room. She was remarkably trim for a woman in her fifties, and to Doc, very attractive.

"Time for a little sponging." She said in perfect English. She turned to Doc, "Would you mind stepping outside, Mr. Ewing?"

Doc laughed, "What the hell for? I've seen everything that kid's got."

Crista smiled, "Those are the rules, Mr. Ewing, but since you used to change his diapers, we'll let it go this time." They all laughed.

"Are you guys fighting over me?" Jon chided airily. He leaned over and patted Crista on the rump," you can change my diapers anytime."

"Sergeant Ewing, how would you like a sponge in the mouth?" she responded and they all laughed again.

Doc watched intently as Nurse Braun proceeded with the bath.

"Do you have a family?" he asked her.

Silence for a moment.

"In memories only." she answered without stopping her chore.

"Oh?" Doc was hesitant to go further.

Crista tenderly washed Jon' wounded leg and continued, "My husband and son were killed in an automobile accident in the summer of 1994. My son, Eric, would have been your age, Jon, had he lived."

This so impacted Jon that he suddenly began to sob. Crista sponged his face and tears away.

"Here now, we'll have none of that. It was nineteen years ago, and time heals wounds."

Jon was calmed by Crista's caresses, but blurted, "It's still a goddamn shitty world."

The remaining time was spent in abject silence.

Nurse Braun finished her task and was collecting her material when Jon grabbed her hand.

"I'm sorry, ma'am. I think I was feeling sorry for myself, plus..... You remind me so much of my mother."

Crista leaned over and kissed Jon's forehead,

"Thank you for such a compliment."

As she was leaving the room, Doc stopped her at the door.

"You also remind me of the women we lost almost twenty years ago....Jon's mother and my wife. Until now, I've never met anyone I could say that about. Thanks for lifting both our spirits."

She left with a smile on her face.

"So you've decided to come back to us." Farid remarked sardonically to Robert as he walked through the side door of the hanger.

"No, not really. I'm just curious about how you intend to pull this all together." Robert responded sweeping an arm toward the laboratory activity.

"You seemed to be a little concerned about my uncle. Would you like to talk to him?"

"That would be an excellent start."

Farid gripped Robert's arm and began walking him toward his uncle.

"I'll need to help with interpretation. Uncle Jahangir has trouble with English."

After the formal introductions, Robert asked.... through Farid....if the uncle was enjoying his stay in the United States. "Very much!" Farid interpreted.

"How long do you intend to stay?" Robert continued.

The uncle stared at Farid as if looking for an appropriate answer. There was a brief exchange between the two before Farid responded.

"He says, ' hopefully, until completion of the project'."

"How long do you think that will be?" Robert asked the uncle. Farid exchanged the question, but to Robert, much longer than it should have taken. Not understanding the language had its disadvantages.

"As long as it takes," Farid translated.

Robert was not sure whether he was getting the answers to his questions from Uncle Jahangir or Farid.

"I'll ask one more.... Your country is considered a state sponsor of terrorism. How did you get a visa to enter the United States?"

Uncle Jahangir's flushed cheeks indicated that he understood all of what Robert had said. The translation bit had been a ruse. Farid, obviously embarrassed by the subterfuge, short-stopped uncle's response.

"My uncle understands some English when he is upset."

Uncle Jahangir burst into high pitched tirade,

"I do not like your friend, Farid. He is unkind. There were many people in our country, I for one, who detest what the terrorist radicals did on that dreadful September day. All Muslims are not bad, young man!"

Robert did not feel compelled to apologize.

"Sometimes it's hard to tell who is and who isn't." He retorted, rubbing in more salt.

"My uncle received his visa through me and my family, who are now American citizens. There are times like this, however, that I am not proud of that fact!"

"It doesn't take much does it, Farid?" With that, Robert left the hanger and walked back to the dorm. Special Agent Holtz was waiting for him in the lobby.

"What did you find out?" Holtz asked as they sat across from each other.

"Not much. This uncle guy is slick. He faked not understanding English, and he and Farid side stepped the truth about his visa. This whole thing stinks."

A student passed through the lobby toward the elevator interrupting their conversation.

Then they were alone again.

"How much credence do you put into the boy's chances of building this thing?" Halted asked.

"None at all, but that's not what I'm thinking about. What happens if Uncle what's-his-name, takes those plans and formulas back to Iran with him where God knows what technical capabilities they have."

Holtz pulled a notebook out of his coat pocket and wrote something down. He looked up at Robert.

"Do you think you can get anything more out of these two?"

"Not a chance. I'm afraid my creditability is shot with them. I doubt if they'd even let me back in the hanger."

"How about the other students on the project?"

Robert responded with a shake of his head,

"I wouldn't know who to trust."

Holtz put his notebook back in his pocket and stood up.

"Thanks for your help, Mr. Gordon. I think our best bet is to keep a tail on the two of them and see where it leads us."

"Can I get back to my studies now. I've got a big exam tomorrow."

Holtz,with a grin on his face and a nod, left the lobby.

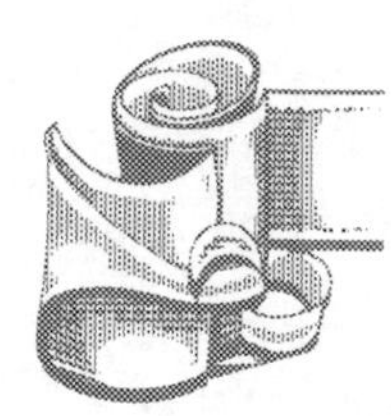

CHAPTER 6

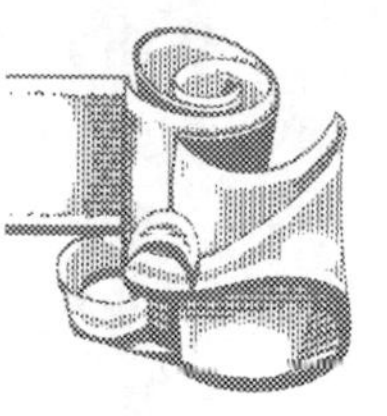

The Russian media were the first to break the Mars story. In the Pravda newspaper:

US FAKES ANOTHER SPACE LANDING!

The moon landing was not enough for the United States. Now they claim they have put a man on the planet Mars.

In the London News:

MAN CLAIMS TO BE ON MARS.

Scientists the world over say the strange voice is definitely emanating from the planet Mars.

UNITED NATIONS

UN blames United States for Mars Ruse. U.S. President denies any connection with the phenomenon.

.....AND ON WCHTV in Chicago:

"We have in our studio this evening, Dr. Ambrose Tavoutaris, Dean of Astronomy at Northwestern University. Doctor, what is your professional opinion of the so-called Mars Man, and could he be, as some experts claim, the missing Gerald Pence and his state-of-the-art aircraft?"

Dr. Tavoutaris chuckled as he answered the question,

"It sounds like a scene from Star Wars, doesn't it? Personally, I think it's some sort of clever ploy."

"You're saying that this whole thing is a joke?"

"Maybe we're going back to the Orson Well's Halloween *War of the Worlds* broadcast of 1938. It sure sounded real at the time and scared a lot of people half to death."

"But, sir, a great many scientists around the world believe the Mars Man story."

"As many of them did in 1938. Much of what this Mr.Pence has said is quite credible, but any of my students could be just as accurate about the planet Mars."

The engineer in the adjoining booth gave the one minute sign.

"We're running out of time, Doctor. Please explain this 'Dark Energy' that was mentioned."

"If I could explain it, I'd be considered a second Einstein. Could it be like a torrent stream in space, that accelerates the speed of a craft when it gets caught up in it as this Mr. Pence claims? Who knows! Not many of us do. Would such a dark energy torrent guide the ship to Mars? It's most unlikely, but his story is intriguing."

The engineer gave the five-second signal.

"Thank you, Dr. Tavoutaris. This is Scott Daniels, WCHTV,"

Steve Gordon sat beside Professor Grant Emerson and Steven, Jr. as they watched early play-backs of the transmissions from Mars. Steve had asked one of Doc Ewing's assistants to take over for him at the Park while he drove to Brooklyn, Indiana and the Goethe Link Observatory. He had arrived early in the afternoon.

Steve shook his head,

"Its hard to believe that Pence's aircraft was capable of this. Most of it's earth-bound feats and maybe a moon shot I can accept, but this.....?"

"Yet all the observatories around the world say the same thing.....these signals are indeed originating form Mars," the Professor responded.

"Remember, Dad, Mr. Pence said the Altair was capable of both space and atmosphere flight." Steven, Jr. added.

"Yes, earth-orbit flight and the moon, but Mars? That's a little hard to swallow."

"It shouldn't be," the Professor said, "with today's technology, we could get there in roughly nine months. How long has Pence been gone?"

"He disappeared in November of last year." Steve answered,"but judging from those play-backs, he's had to have reached there a lot sooner than nine months. He sounds too settled in to have just arrived."

"If this is a hoax, Professor, how could Pence have made his messages seem like they were coming from Mars." Steven, Jr. asked.

"Many ways, young man. I'm not saying that I agree it's a hoax, but there are many ways someone with the technological knowledge could do it."

The professor walked to an tablet easel board, took a marker from the tray and began drawing a series of circles radiating from one large one in the center.

"Let me demonstrate," He pointed to the large circle, "this is Mars." He drew several small squares on the Mars circle, "These are the rovers that exist on the planet now. One is the Russian Mars 1, and the other two are the USA Viking 1, and 2. The Mars 1 was destroyed on landing. Both Vikings landed safely and as far as we know are functioning and capable of relaying messages between Mars and Earth." He drew circles around the outer rings, "These are several existing orbiters. All of them also capable of exchanging communications with Mother Earth. In either of these cases, anyone with the know-how could bounce messages from earth to the orbiters and back to earth again and make it seem like it was coming from Mars."

"What do you think, Professor?" Steve asked.

"I've been timing these transmissions and they all fall into the same period of time here. Wherever this Mr. Pence and his vehicle are located, the messages come at the same time period when that location faces the earth."

"So, you're saying the transmission are coming from the surface of Mars, not from orbit."

"Precisely! The timing would indicate that." the professor answered.

Steven, Jr. interjected, "Haven't the other observatories figured that out?"

"I imagine they have, but it doesn't prove that it is or isn't a hoax."

Steve stood up and slipped into his jacket.

"I think it's a cute little game this guy is playing. He's very clever. I still think he's basking in the sunlight of some remote South Pacific island having the time of his life."

Crista and Doc sat across from each other in the hospital cafeteria. Both eating hamburgers. Doc held his up.

"I guess we can thank your country for starting all this."

"But it took you people to make it popular." Crista grinned, took a bite and chewed.

"Anyway, it makes me feel right at home here in Frankfurt. Did they invent the hot dog?"

They both laughed, then grew serious.

"Do you have any family at all here?" Doc asked.

Crista, shook her head,

"Not here. My closest relative is my brother, Frank, and he lives in San Francisco in the good old USA."

Doc brightened,

"So it wouldn't be hard for you to come to live in the.... good old USA?"

"Not if I wanted to." Crista returned.

"You mean you don't?" Doc's voice sank.

Both finished their hamburgers and sat silently sipping their coffee. Criata weighed her response.

"I've got a good job here. I've got some aunts and uncles scattered around Germany that I occasionally visit. Oh, I get lonely at times, I'll admit that, but my memories are still here."

Doc let this sink in for several seconds and then reached out for her hand. She did not withdraw it.

"Crista, you remember my comment the other day, about meeting someone that reminded me of the woman I lost many years ago?"

She smiled,

"Yes I do. It was very kind."

"Please think of it not as a kindness, but as a confession. I never thought I could love another woman until now. What I was confessing is that now.... I have met that woman."

Crista blushed and quivered a smile.

"They say that the patient most always falls in love with the nurse,"

She said softly.

"But I'm not the patient. Just maybe a little love sick," he grinned.

She squeezed his hand.

"What are you trying to say?"

"Jon and I will be returning the States soon, maybe within the next two weeks. It would break my heart if I left without knowing if you'd be willing to start new memories with me."

"Is this a proposal, Doc?"

He nodded his head and squeezed her hand back. They were both silent. Then she glanced at her watch.

"I'd better be getting back. I'm on hospital time now."

"No answer?" was Doc's response.

She leaned across the table and kissed him on the forehead.

"Not now." she whispered, and left.

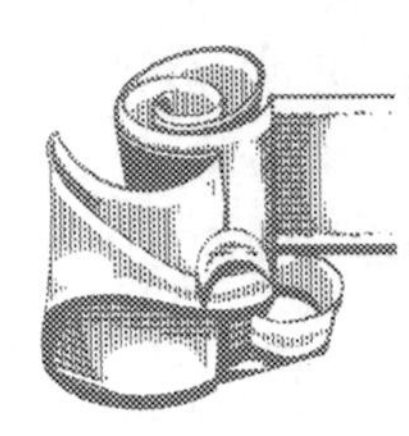

CHAPTER 7

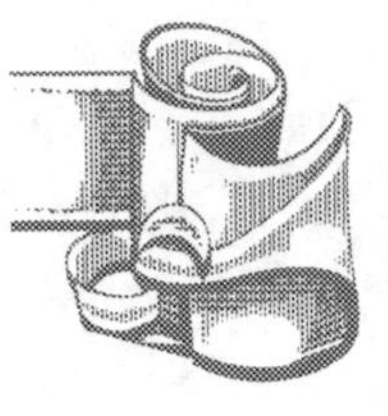

Mars
10/ 11/'03

"Our food supply was running low until we converted part of our pantry into a greenhouse and were able to supplement what food supplies we had left in our pantry with the vegetables we've grown. Janet has become quite a creative cook with all this. Most of her meals are tasty and nutritious.We've discovered that the water in the subterranean lake is drinkable albeit quite sulphuric in taste.

The black creatures around the lake keep running away when I flash my light on them, so I can't make out yet what they are.

Janet is calling me to dinner. We're having what she calls Martian Goulash.

Will transmit later."

The professor turned to his students behind him and shook his head.

"It sounds as though they're having too much fun...where ever they are."

Robert wasn't surprised that Farid had left the dorm, but he was astonished at how quickly he got a new roommate. He was tall, dark and yes, handsome. Not typical of the short, stocky, thick necked Hispanic. His name was Hugo Munoz, and he demonstrated a keen sense of humor.

"My great grandfather ran a sword through David Crockett at the Alamo." He said with a straight face.

Robert retorted,

"No one knows how David Crockett died that day."

"Well, now you know!"

Hugo's baritone voice was a contrast to Farid's s tenor voice, and in all respects, Robert was quite pleased with his new roommate. Hugo was majoring in Criminal Justice, and since there were some similar subjects in Robert's major of Aeronautical Engineering, they had the opportunity to exchange ideas. Hugo was from Austin Texas, and had gone one year at Texas A&M, but transferred to Purdue because of what he thought was a better curriculum structure and also because he had relatives close to West Lafayette. Anyway, they got along, and there was no talk of insane ideas or projects.

Steve returned home from the park in the early evening and took Becky's message off call waiting. He noted that the area code she had called from was out of state. That was confusing.

The phone rang and he anxiously picked it up.

"Hi Pop, I just wanted to fill you in on what's happened since I've talked to you last."

"Make it quick," Steve said, " I'm expecting another call."

"Okay...The Iranian guy is no longer my roommate. My new one is great and I've gotten out of this crazy aircraft project. How's that for quick?"

"What about this guy's uncle you where so concerned about?"

"I've got the FBI on him." a smug return from Robert.

"FBI! My God, Robert, what have you gotten yourself into?"

Steve grew more anxious.

"Don't worry, Dad, I've backed away from that too."

"Robert, you haven't learned, have you? Once you stick your head in FBI business, you don't back away!"

Call waiting clicked.

"My expected call is coming in....I'll call you back...and stay in your room until I do. I want to talk to you more about this whole thing."

They hung up, and the other call rang through. It was Becky.

Robert clicked off his cell phone and sat staring at it.

"I think I'm in deep shit! The old man is pissed."

Hugo looked up from his law text.

"What's the problem?"

Robert told the whole story of Gerald Pence, his disappearance in the Altair and Farid's efforts to build another one..

Hugo shook his head,

"I've heard about that Farid nut, but the Mars story is something else. Do you really believe that Pence guy is up there?"

"I know my dad doesn't, but there's apparently a lot of people who do.."

"And you wouldn't believe my Alamo story." Hugo chuckled.

Robert's cell phone jingled. He answered and listened in silence.

"Are you sure of all this?" he said. He listened again, and finally...."Thanks."and hung up. He sat deep in thought. Hugo looked on curiously.

"Now what?"

"This is the night of the long knives! The Purdue administration has shut down all Raisbeck Engineering associated with the experimental aircraft project Farid was working on. All aeronautical students involved have been recalled, and according to this guy that called, Farid has left the University."

"What about the uncle and those plans?" Hugo asked.

"That's what scares me. If Farid is gone, it follows that his uncle is gone too with both the plans and the formulas."

"Back to Iran?"

"God, I hope not!" Robert responded.

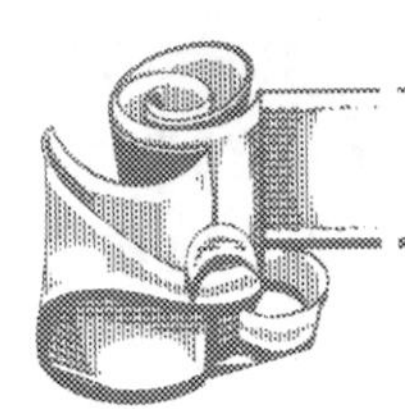

CHAPTER 8

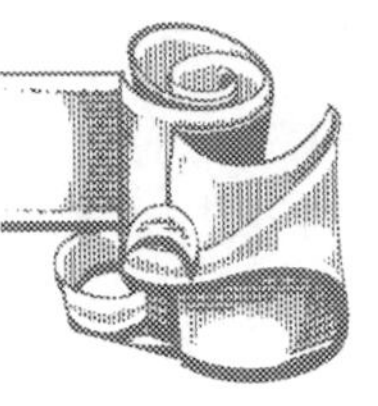

"What are you doing in California?" Steve asked trying to hide his irritation.

"NASSA's Jet Propulsion laboratory called me yesterday afternoon and asked if I'd be willing to fly out here to help with communications with Dad. I couldn't say no, so they sent a private jet and I flew out of Indianapolis International later that evening. Steve, I talked to him....I talked to Dad early this morning." Becky said with ebullience.

Steve could hear himself breathing in the phone. Then.....

"So, what did he have to say?"

"It took several tries before we could make connections. Apparently, an orbiter has to be in the right position to receive messages from the surface. Then the relay to earth takes about four minutes The same is true in reverse. The problem is that the surface message has only three minutes to relay its message before the orbiter is out of range."

"You lost me somewhere back there! Just tell me what was said," Steve begged.

"He asked about you, and the two of us. I lied to him and said everything was fine..."

Steve interrupted, "What do you mean *lied?* Are you trying to tell me something?"

"Steve, let's not get into that. We can talk about our personal problems later."

Steve wasn't satisfied with Becky's answer but let her continue.

"He repeated some of the things he's been saying to the world, and.....wished I was there!" She giggled, "Then the connection went bad. The people at the Laboratory told me that the orbiter camera showed a large dust storm developing in the area where he's supposed to be and they attributed the cut off to that."

"You believe he's really up there, don't you?"

"So do millions of other people. Don't you?"

"That's another thing we'll talk about. When are you coming back?" Steve asked eagerly.

" I should be in Indianapolis tomorrow afternoon." she responded.

"Not Indianapolis....here in Williams Creek!"

There was a long pause.

"Do you want me there?"

Steve half scolded and half laughed.

"Oh come on, Becky. You get your butt back her where you belong, on the double!"

Becky's voice brightened.

"Okay, okay, Masta! Oh, by the way, before I lost connections with Dad, he told me Janet was pregnant."

Steven, Jr. was having trouble concentrating on his post-graduate studies. What the hell does an intensified accounting class have to do with Environmental Engineering, he asked himself. I'm not planning on being an accountant, heaven forbid. Why do I have to do this corporate financial mock-up stuff anyway?

He was concerned about the relationship between his father and Becky. He was unable to rationalize his father's inability to break away from the memory of his deceased mother. He was concerned about his growing doubts over the validity of Gerald Pence's existence on Mars. He was especially concerned over the break-up with his girl friend, Jessica, the 'Cute Couple' on campus. He was buzzing mentally, and accounting was tremendously out of place. He stood up, stretched and grabbed his jacket. A walk would do him good.

It was early October and a crisp evening. The street lights had just come on and the usual bustle of a college campus had come to a crawl. Parents Day was two days off, highlighted by the Illinois/Indiana football game. Steven decided to walk to Memorial Stadium just blocks away.

He stood staring at the vast structure with its empty seats, and ghostly memories of games gone-by. His thoughts focused on his father who had played line-backer for the Illini from 1972 through 1974. He imagined the roar of the crowd that September afternoon in 1973, the only time his father had played here at Memorial Stadium. Illinois had won that one 28-14, and his father had been awarded the game ball for outstanding play.

He walked onto the field, climbed into the stands and up to the top of the stadium and sat down.

With the clearness of the evening came the array of bright stars in the sky. Which one was Mars, he thought. The slightly red one there? Yes, that had to be it. In the progression closest to earth, it was extraordinarily bright. Was Gerald Pence up there?

He shook his head, and switched his thoughts back to earth and his years at Indiana University. He had been rushed by three fraternities in his freshman year—Alpha Tau Omega, Sigma Chi, and Lambda Chi Alpha, but elected to stay independent, at least for his first year. He remained independent for rest of his undergraduate years. In his sophomore year, it was here at Memorial Stadium that he had met Jessica. He couldn't remember what team they played, or who won, but remembered the cute little freshman girl sitting in front of him. She was a petite four foot eight inches tall, and Steven's six foot two inches made them the campus, 'Cute Couple'. They dated through his senior year, but when his mother died prior to his graduation, the relationship began unraveling. They both tried hard to preserve it all, but Steven found it difficult to control his despair. He had changed. She had been patient and understanding at first, but began to realize the fruitlessness of it. She began dating other boys and the 'Cute Couple' sobriquet became a thing of the past.

Steven sat there for perhaps twenty minutes more, staring down at the empty field, and watching an occasional student walk by.

I hate accounting, he thought, but if I'm going to get my Masters, I'd better choke it down. He got up and walked back to his studies.

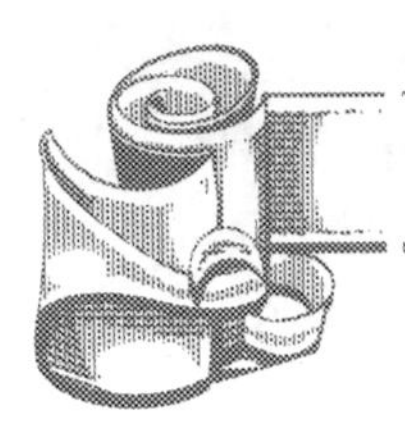

CHAPTER 9

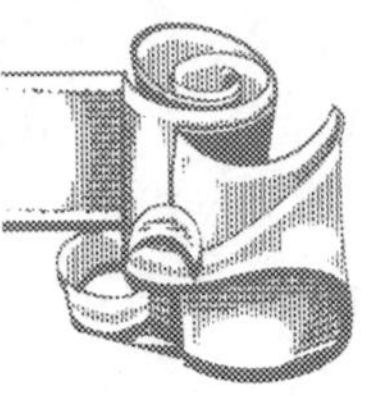

Robert's efforts to get hold of FBI Agent Hal Holtz, against his father's advise, proved futile. So he invited his roommate, Hugo, to join him in an excursion to the supposedly abandoned hanger at Purdue's Airport.

There were several campus police guarding the front of the building, so they cautiously slipped around to the back. Hugo was getting nervous.

"If we get caught, senior," he whispered in feigned Mexican accent, "we go to the gallows."

Robert suppressed a laugh.

"There's got to be a way to get in here. Let's try some back windows." he mumbled.

"I've always wondered why you Americans insist on Santa Claus coming down a chimney, when to us, coming through the door makes more sense." Still in Mexican accent.

"Get serious, dammit!" Robert rasped, but tried the back door anyway. It opened.

"See, this Mexican Santa Claus, he one smart cookie." Hugo continued the act.

Robert, in exasperation, shoved Hugo through the opened door.The interior was not entirely empty. The framework of the fuselage was still on the platform, and the main line computer was still sitting in a corner close to the door.

"For God's sake," Robert whispered, " why did they leave the computer behind?"

"Maybe it didn't contain what they wanted." Hugo responded.

"What do you mean?" Robert shot back.

"I'm betting that since it came from Mr. Pence's office, all it contained is administrative stuff. Nothing pertaining to this Altair....Senior."

"Cut that out, Hugo!" Robert shouted in disgust.

Robert studied the fuselage framework.

"This is nothing but a wooden frame!"

"A decoy, maybe?" Hugo ventured.

The hydraulic front hanger door began opening. The startled Hugo and Robert ran to the back and out the door. They crouched and waited on the outside as three figures entered through the partially opened hanger door. Their voices were muffled so neither Robert or Hugo could make out what they were saying. Then one figure came to the computer close to the door.

"I think we need to move this out, and study its contents."

Robert recognized the voice, and jumped up and back into the hanger.

"Mr. Holtz, I've been trying to get hold of you all morning!"

He shouted, his voice echoing in the vastness of the hanger.

Holtz flashed a light toward Robert.

"Yes, I know. I got your message from our call waiting, and since you mentioned the hanger, I figured this is where you'd be." He turned to the two security guards and waved them off.

"It's okay, gentlemen, these boys are working with me."

"Are you aware of what's been happening?" Robert interjected.

"Oh, yes, your roommate here informed me of everything. Mr. Gordon, meet intern agent, Hugo Munoz."

Hugo bowed deeply in true courtly fashion.

"My pleasure, Senior."

"Son-of-a-bitch!" Robert blurted, "You can't trust anybody!"

Jon and Doc were waiting in their hospital room for the release papers from the doctor. They were homeward bound within hours.

Nurse Crista Braun entered the room. Her eyes were red. She had been crying and it was noticeable.

"Tears?" Doc quietly asked.

She dabbed her eyes and grinned.

"Just a little cold. I see that you both are ready to leave us. What a disappointment that will be."

Doc handed her a kleenex,

"I know how miserable head colds can be this time of year. I have a slight one myself." He pulled another kleenex from the box and blew his nose. They stood silently studying one another as the doctor cheerfully entered the room with the release papers.

"You are free to go my brave friends. We will miss you." the doctor glowed. "There is a military limousine waiting to take you to the airport. Auf wiederschen my dear friends." The doctor bowed and left the room.

Jon wrestled with his newly procured crutches as he wobbled to his feet. Doc placed his hands on Crista's shoulders.

"Still no answer?" He asked.

The tears came freely now.

"Oh my dear soul, I wish I had one. But for now it is also auf wiedershen."

They left the room. Crista cupped her hands over her face and wept with abandonment.

Jon and Doc boarded the AN-12 Transport at the Frankfurt Airport, both feeling that something dear was being left behind.

As the plane began rolling away from the gate, Doc looked forlornly at the faces in the crowd by the terminal. She was not there. He didn't expect her to be, but there was that hope. As the plane taxied to the take off runway, Doc finally accepted the fact, although reluctantly, that there might never be an answer.

It had been just a little less than an hour when the transport landed in London to take on some personnel, provisions and fuel. It departed London a half-hour later and was soon droning over the Atlantic Ocean.

A United States Marine Colonel, who had boarded the plane in London, approached Doc and Jon.

" Staff Sergeant Jon Ewing?" he asked.

Jon's seat had been turned down so he could sleep, which he was doing at that moment. Doc answered, "Yes, I'm his father."

The Colonel handed Doc a telegram.

"This is from Washington, sir. Would you give it to the sergeant when he awakens."

"Certainly," Doc answered. He studied the envelope curiously and was almost tempted to open it, but didn't.

The plane droned on.

"Go ahead and open it, Dad, and read it to me. They're probably drafting me," Jon said, having wakened from his nap.

Doc tore open the envelope and read the contents:

Staff Sergeant Jon D. Ewing,

It is the pleasure of The President of The United States of America to request your presence at the White House immediately upon your arrival at the nation's capital.

Best regards,
George.W. Simmons
President of the United States of America

"What the hell is that all about?" Jon asked.

Before Doc could offer an opinion, the marine colonel approached them again, stopped and saluted Jon.

"I have been given permission to inform you, Sergeant, that the President will present you with the Congressional Medal of Honor. On behalf of the Marine Corps, and the United States of America, we are very proud and extend our congratulations!"

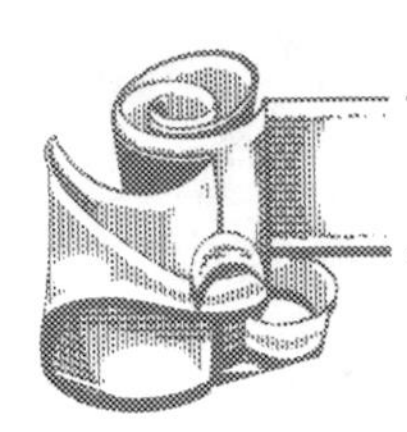

CHAPTER 10

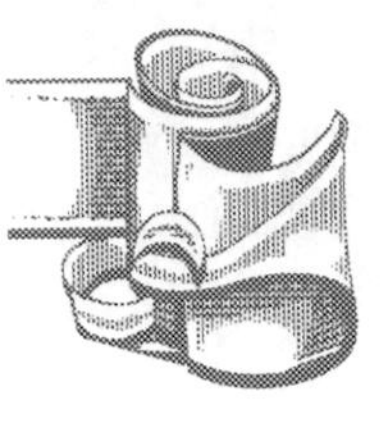

Mars
11/11/'03

"A severe dust storm has come up outside our cave. The wind must be well over one-hundred miles per hour. It's so strong that the mouth of the cave howls like the sound made by blowing on the lip of an empty coke bottle. We were forced to stay inside the Altair to reduce the piercing sound and also the swirling dust.

I got a better look at our black creatures this morning. For the life of me they look like giant cockroaches. I've heard that they are considered the lobster of the land. I can't wait to catch one and see if it's true.

It has crossed my mind that we can't stay on Mars forever. I am working with the computer to determine when it would be possible for an attempt to return to earth. It would seem that the big problem is to slip back into whatever it was that brought us here. Right now, as I transmit, the

Mars dust is piling up against the cave entrance, and closing us in. We may have a problem."

The word from The Arizona University Observatory to Professor Emerson was that there was indeed a massive dust storm on Mars at the time of the last transmission.The professor shook his head. There was no way that Pence could know that unless he was there. Also it was difficult to imagine that he would have concocted the ridiculous cockroach story if he hadn't seen them there.

What to believe, the professor agonized, what to believe.

Becky's plane from California landed on time at the Indianapolis International, and Steve waited anxiously for her to come through the passenger gate. When she appeared, they embraced, to the delight of the surrounding crowd. She got her bags, and they left for their home in Park View, outside of the state park. On their way, after some idle chatter, Steve told Becky that Doc Ewing had called from Washington,D.C., just before he left to pick her up. He was returning the day after tomorrow. He mentioned that Jon was awarded the Medal Of Honor, and was assigned to Walter Reed Hospital for extensive physical therapy for probably a six month period....probably not that long, knowing Jon. But, Steve said, that for some reason, Doc didn't sound as cheerful as you would expect under the circumstances. Perhaps he was just exhausted, Becky offered. Yes, Perhaps that was it.

Steven, Jr. ran into Jessica in the IU Main Library in early November. They sat at different tables for as long as they could pretend not to notice each other.

Steven gave in. He walked over to Jessica's table and sat down in front of her. She kept her eyes on her book until Steve reached over and closed it. That provoked a temporary staring match, until Steven spoke.

"Still dating what's his name?" he asked sarcastically.

She looked up with a smile and reopened the page she was on.

"I'm not dating these days. What about you.?"

"I haven't seen anybody since I graduated last spring."

Finally, Steven reached over and took hold of Jessica's hand.

"Things haven't been easy for me these days." He said, " I've found myself stewing over things, knowing full well that there isn't much I can do about them. But I've never stopped thinking about us."

The library closing bell rang. It was time to go, but Steven and Jessica stretched it out.

"What are your plans after you graduate next Spring?" Steven asked.

"I will probably go for my Masters, as you've done...or I'll teach for awhile and then go for my Masters."

"Sounds like a great plan. I'd go for your Masters right away while your study habits are still intact."

The librarian approached the two, "I'm sorry, the Library is now closed for the evening. You will have to leave."

They nodded and left.

It was a long walk from the library on tenth street to the Pi Beta Phi house on third street, but the evening was mild for the month of November, and was a comfortable walk for both. Steven and Jessica were silent for a great part of the time, each steeped in their individual thoughts. They passed a bench just outside Jessica's sorority house, and sat down.

"Why do they always have street lights over benches?" Steven lightly inquired.

They sat nervously for moments, then Steven took Jessica's hand.

"We've had a lot of good times together, you and I."

"Yes, we have, and I've missed them." Jessica shyly responded, She pondered the thought and then spoke up."What was the best time you can remember?"

Steven thought for a moment.

"I guess it would be when I spent Thanksgiving with you and your family...and your snot nosed little brother."

Jessica laughed,

"You got along so well with them all. You are so tall Dad thought surely you played basketball for IU."

"I had a tough time explaining that it takes a great deal of coordination to play that sport, which I don't have much of."

"Your dad was a good football player."

"Yes, indeed, but that's one thing I didn't inherit from him."

"What did you inherit from him?"

"Let's see... Stubbornness, maybe a little intelligence. Most intelligence I do have though, I got from my Mother."

Jessica sobered.

"Have you learned to cope with her passing?"

"I'm trying very hard, but you only have one true mother in life, and most of your memories hinge on her and her loving care. When that suddenly goes away, it leaves a horrible vacuum."

There was silence after that. Presently Jessica stood up.

"I think I'd better go. It's almost curfew time."

Steven reached up and pulled her back down on the bench.

"Could we be the 'Cute Couple' again?"

"I was hoping you'd say that."

They embraced.

"Goodnight." Jessica whispered.

Kyle Broyles was Special FBI Agent for the Indianapolis area. In cooperation with Agent Hal Holtz, they arranged to meet at the vacant Gerald Pence Technology Corporation office building in Indianapolis.They wanted to search the interior. Hugo Munoz was with them.

They discovered the means of entrance by the debris on the floor of Pence's office. The clean-up on the roof of the building was skillfully executed by the thieves, leaving no clues. The whole affair was brazen, and it was incredible that all this was done unobserved.

Agent Broyles had been involved in the Gerald Pence affair and the development of the aircraft called the Altair, in Arabic, meaning 'Flying Eagle'. This all led to two murders and the death of the two antagonists responsible for those murders. It also led to the reassignment of

Broyle's cohort out of the Chicago office, Special Agent Chuck Manning. because of his aggressive and misdirected attempt to procure the plans of the craft for the US government.

The three of them browsed the office and found nothing that would give them any further clues.

"Whoever is responsible for all this, knew what the hell he...or she...was doing," Holtz commented.

"It's ironic that after they went to all this trouble, the mainframe turned out to be of no value to them," Broyles smiled.

"But now the big question is, where did they go when they left the hanger at Purdue?" Holtz mused.

The group vacated and locked up the building. Nothing had been accomplished.

The two agents and Hugo sat in one of the cars summing up their thoughts.

"According to the young Gordon boy, Pence had given the Iranian the plans and formulas for this Altair." Broyles observed, "but for the life of me, I can't figure out why."

"This Pence guy was something else. For whatever reason, it was for a purpose. Maybe, sooner or later, we'll know what it was," Holtz concluded.

They all went their separate ways.

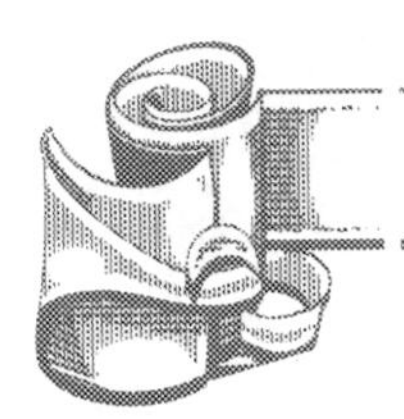

CHAPTER 11

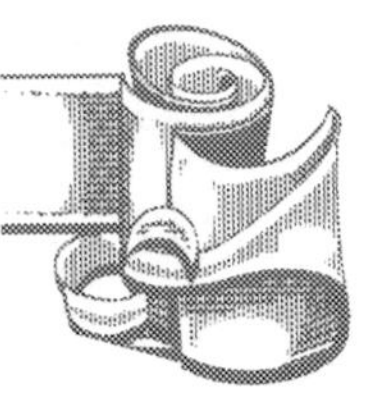

The relationship between Robert and Hugo drastically changed since it became known he was an FBI intern. Conversation was now tentative.

Robert remembered his father's exhortation to steer shy of becoming involved in FBI business. He was not about to tell his dad what his new roommate had turned out to be. Rooming with a potential FBI Agent.... I'd get pulled out of school for sure, he thought.

So the evenings at study became very quiet. Finally, after the third day following the tour of the empty hanger, Hugo closed his book and looked over at Robert.

"You're pissed because I've chosen to go with the FBI? It's a great profession...you ought to consider it."

"It's the deception that bothers me. Why the hell didn't you come right out and tell me when you first got here?"

Hugo laughed,

"Because being sneaky is part of the curriculum. I just wanted to see how long it would take to be discovered. That's the fun of it."

Robert became deep in thought.

"If I decided to go FBI, my dad would disown me."

"I think you're exaggerating." Hugo smirked.

"No, I'm not. You guys are like bulldogs. Once you latch on to something, you don't let go. We've had plenty of experience with that. That's the point my dad is trying to make."

"Winston Churchill was the world's worst bulldog and he saved England."

"Churchill didn't save England. The *people* saved England!" Robert retorted loudly.

"He was the teeth that hung on!" Hugo answered going for the last word.

Robert went back to his studies, "Subject closed."

After a half hour of silence, Hugo stood up, walked to the window and surveyed what view they had of the campus.

"You have to have a keen sense of intuitiveness to be a good agent," he muttered.

"I suppose you have that in abundance," Robert returned without looking up from his text book.

"I have my share of it." He walked back to his desk." You want to know what I think?"

"About what?" Robert gave up his studying

"I have a hunch that the Altair plans and formulas may not be here on earth. I think, that for what ever reason Pence had, he gave this Farid kid a bunch of crap. *If* Pence *is* on Mars, that's where they are...safe and sound."

"Boy, you may not be intuitive, but you have one hell of an imagination. Where do you get all this?"

"This was a light class day for me so I had the chance to go to Indianapolis with Agent Holtz this morning to search Pence's old office building for clues on who hoisted the mainframe."

"So?"

"I don't know if this means anything, but I noticed the serial number on the power cord in Pence's office, and then I compared it with the serial number of the mainframe here."

"So?"

"They didn't match."

"So"?

Hugo pondered Robert's response,

"Maybe you're right, the FBI is not for you."

Robert's patience was running thin.

"Get to the point!"

"If a power cord's serial number typically should match the machine it's attached to, then the mainframe they took from Pence's office is not the original unit. If that's the case, then it follows that the plans and formulas he gave Farid may be phony too."

"That's your intuitiveness?"

"Just a hunch."

"Don't tell Holtz. He'll fire your ass."

The media around the world continued to treat the "Mars Man" story with ridicule and contempt. Russia was suddenly an exception. It was forbidden there to print or air anything concerning it.

Satirizing editorial cartoons and articles were plentiful everywhere. A London journal even began a comic strip entitled "Mars Man," and it became an overwhelming hit in Europe. The world was having fun with the Man on Mars.

Becky was a victim of it all. She was the daughter of that man. She had supposedly talked to him from there.The media wasn't structured to ignore the editorial possibilities. Steve was grateful that she had returned. The boys were ecstatic that their 'Becky Mom', as they called her, was back, but the media people were constantly underfoot. National and world-wide magazines, television stations, including several late night programs, and newspapers all wanted to interview her. Time, Life and Newsweek magazines wanted to make her their cover girl. It was terrifying to Becky, and irritating to Steve. Not a moment of peace.

"Why don't I just leave? Maybe they won't bother you guys," she said sorrowfully.

"Don't you even think about it." Steve barked, "We'll ride this whole ridiculous thing out one way or another."

To the delight of Steven, Jr. And Robert, the wedding had been reset for December 15....in concrete..... And if he would accept, Doc was to be best man.

CHAPTER 12

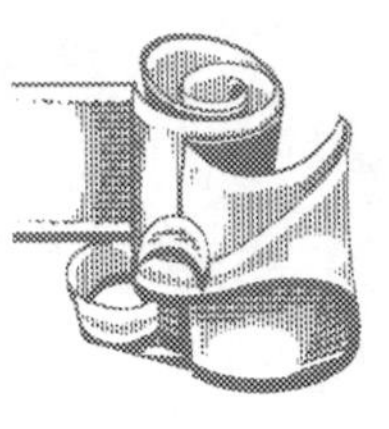

Mars

11/23/ 03

"The dust storm has subsided and probably will end soon. Our cave entrance almost completely sealed, but I intend to turn the Altair afterburners on it to blast the loose silt away. I see no problem.

I suppose you'll see Thanksgiving shortly before we do, because Mar's days are about forty minutes longer than yours.You'll will be eating turkey, and if I can, in the next several days, capture one of those black things, we'll be having that. As I've said, Janet, my companion, has turned into quite a chef. I'm losing a little weight, but Janet seems to be gaining. I wonder why.

I'm still working with the computer to construct a program for getting back to Earth. If worse comes to worse, we'll load up on hydrogen fuel, extracted from the water in our lake, and black bugs" to supplement our food supply, and fly home without the slipstream or whatever got us here.

Will check in later."

Doc checked into his home outside of Williams Creek and then came to the office. Steve was there and rose to greet his boss as he entered.

"You look tired," Steve suggested.

"A little jet lag....it's been quite an experience.... but I'll be okay. How'd things go?"

"Pretty non plus. No lost hunters or murders. It was rather boring." Steve joked, "How's Jon?"

"Well, you're looking at a pretty proud papa. I don't know where that guy gets all his heroic stuff, but he sure's got it." Doc gleamed.

"He's a chip off the old block, as they say. When do you think they'll release him from Walter Reed?"

Doc sat at his desk and noted that it was about as clean as he'd ever seen it. Steve poured two styrofoam cups of coffee and delivered them to the desk. He sat down across from Doc.

Doc picked up on the question.

"It won't take any six months, I'm betting. They'll be giving him a prosthetic lower limb, which will be the thing that will take up most of the rehab. He'll be able to walk naturally, and with long trousers you won't be able to tell it's artificial." he sipped his coffee.

"That's great." Steve smiled.

"....And how are you and Becky coming along?" Doc ventured.

"You were right about how Becky would take another postponement. We separated for awhile, but we're back together and planning the wedding for December 15. We want you to be best man."

"I'll say yes, if there are no more postponements."

"It's all locked in concrete."

"Great... I'd be honored."

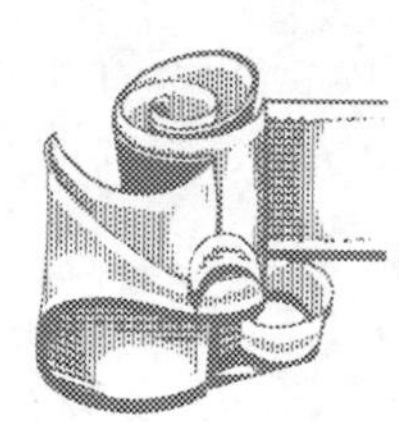

CHAPTER 13

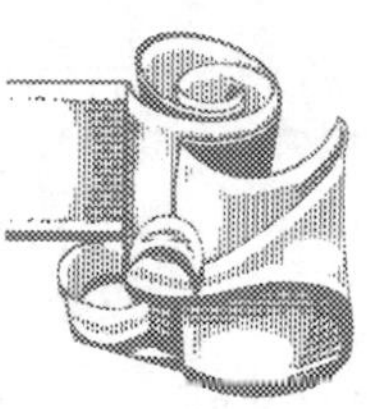

Uncle Jahangir and Farid sat in their room at The Holiday Express Inn outside the Indianapolis International Airport. Uncle Jahangir looked at his watch as he sipped his beer.

"We have another half hour before the shuttle pick-up. It will be good to get home."

"Home to you....not to me," Farid responded nervously.

"Tell me again, why did my mother and father go back to Iran?"

Another sip of beer and Uncle answered, "To visit a sick relative, my nephew."

"I can't think of what relative would be important enough to make them willing to go back to that treacherous country," Farid complained.

"I wouldn't worry about that. In any case, they will be glad to see you, as will our laboratory."

"Laboratory?"

"If they won't allow us to build our aircraft here in the United States, we'll build it in our country."

"Build it with what?" Farid barked."The so called mainframe was a dud, and Pence's plans and formulas didn't make any sense."

"You have no faith, Nephew. The plans, formulas, and mainframe made sense before I changed them," Uncle continued over Farid's attempt to interrupt, "and the computer material is well in hand."

Farid shook his head in exasperation.

"What do you mean?"

Jahangir got up from his chair and walked over to his clothing bag thrown across the bed. He graced it with a sweep of his hand.

"This, my dear nephew, is the mainframe information, and the plans!"

Farid was dumbfounded. Uncle laughed.

"You are not the only genius, my boy." He pulled out a jacket from the bag, "There are miniaturized computer chips and operational ingredients sewn into the fabric of this coat with enough capacity to carry both the plans and everything the main frame contained. All of what we need to develop and improve Mr. Pence's 'Altair'.....and the airport baggage screeners will never detect it! "

The phone rang. It was the desk clerk informing Jahangir that the shuttle was ready to take them to the airport.

"Our adventure now begins! Our great land of Aryans will yet rule the sky!" Uncle said as he picked up the baggage and waved his nephew toward the door.

Becky received an e-mail message from Steven, Jr.

Becky Mom & Dad,

I'd like to bring Jessica home for Thanksgiving tomorrow. Is that Okay?

Steven

She responded.

Of course you can. She can stay as long as she wants.

Love,
Becky Mom

Shortly afterwards, Robert e-mailed.

I'm bringing my roommate home for Thanksgiving. I Hope that's okay.

Robert

Steve and Becky sat across from each other at the kitchen table. Becky was taking notes.

"I hope our turkey is big enough. We're having seven for Thanksgiving dinner which includes the kids..their friends, you and I and Doc."

Steve laughed, "and I thought the twenty-four pound one was be too big."

It would be a happy Thanksgiving occasion, except for Doc. There was clearly something on his mind.He would be there and *try* to be sociable. Steve was determined to talk to Doc sometime soon.

Becky and Steve spent the evening preparing for the next day's dinner. Steve was working on the dressing, Becky on the pies and cleaning up the twenty-four pound turkey.

"I'll make the mashed potatoes tomorrow," Steve said, "that's one thing you can't do properly a day in advance."

Becky nodded her head.

"Let's see.... I think two pumpkin pies, one walnut and one sugar pie should be enough."

Steve laughed, " I would think so!"

There was a period of silence as the two pursued their assignments. Becky put the pumpkin pies in the oven and returned to where Steve was finishing up dicing the celery.

"I only wish Dad and Janet were here." She yearned.

"It'd be one hell of a long sleigh ride, if they really were up there."

"You really don't think they are, do you?" Becky said with a bit of pique.

Steve scraped the celery into the bowl of bread crumbs.

"I can't get it through my thick head that your dad could do what learned scientist say will take a decade to do....put men on Mars.. Then when and if that ever happens, to try to convert the dead planet into a livable place. I'm sorry, honey, it's nothing against your dad, but all of this is quite unbelievable, and is causing quite a stir down here for you and the family....and for the rest of the world for that matter. I'd really like to think it's true, but I don't."

Both of them wanted to avoid an argument so they remained quiet for a period. Then Steve concluded his thoughts by kissing Becky on the forehead.

"Yeah, I wish they were here too."

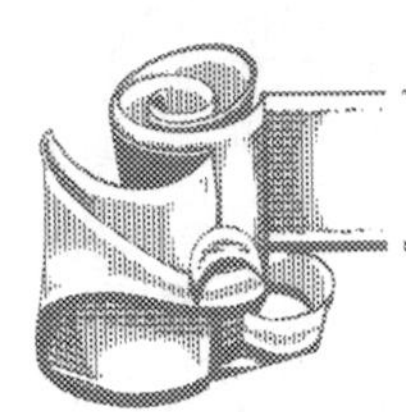

CHAPTER 14

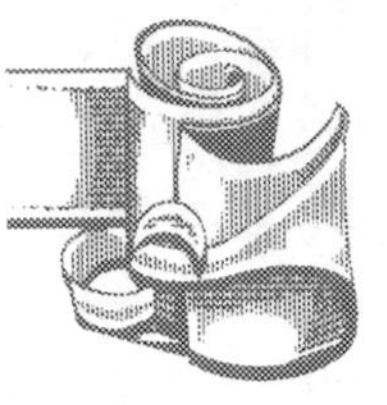

Hugo and Robert stepped under the **NO TRESPASSING** tape in front of the abandoned hanger and entered through the front door.

Robert complained, "How many more times do you have to case this place before you're convinced there's nothing here?"

"Patience is the staff of life, Amigo," Hugo grinned.

At first glance, nothing had seemed to change. The mainframe was still in its corner and the adjoining glassed-in area had not taken on any new appearances.

"Let's just look around one more time, You take the glass-in, I'll check out the mainframe again." They separated.

The sound of an approaching airliner roared overhead, then the squeal of rubber against the runway. Traffic would be picking up this time of the year, with students leaving for home to have their Thanksgiving dinners with their families. It was a short break, dampened by the thought of semester exams the following week. It was the Christmas break they all looked forward to. Robert called to Hugo, " There's a bunch of stuff on the floor in here. Come take a look."

"Computer chips casings." Hugo observed.

"What does that say to your intuition, Mr. Intern?"

Hugo picked several off the floor and examined them closely.

"It means some sort of computer activity may have been going on in here. Disassemble and or reassemble maybe."

"So?'

"I don't know. I'll have to think on this one." Hugo leaned over and picked up a large plastic bag which had been tossed in the corner.Copy on it read, *Wallies Dry Cleaning, 24 hour service.*

Becky had the seating all arranged. Steve would sit at one end of the table, and Doc at the other. To Steve's right would be Becky, then Steven, Jr., and Jessica. To the left would be Hugo, and then Robert. In front of Steve was the huge 24 pound turkey ready to be carved. There was a stack of seven plates, and around that, all the ingredients for a fine Thanksgiving meal. Steve was to carve the turkey, fill each plate and pass it down to a waiting dinner member. It had always been a tradition in Steve's family to serve that way. It would continue with his new family.

An appropriate grace was said, with each of the participants holding hands. That too was a tradition. Steve wanted to assure that each member present was suitably covered in the blessing, so it was quite lengthy.

At "Amen", Robert blurted, "...and please God, keep the mashed potatoes warm." That drew a laugh and the meal began on a waggish tone.

Dessert was served and coffee for those who wanted it, and the Thanksgiving meal was over.

In a moment of silence, Hugo leaned toward Steve.

"I understand you have a problem with the FBI, sir," he said.

Robert cringed and elbowed Hugo.

"Problem? I have no doubt that Robert has told you about the experience we had last year involving Gerald Pence, his magic machine and the FBI. I realize they have a job to do, but I didn't like the way some of their agents went about it."

"Yes, I heard about the dreadful antics of special agent Manning during that time. Inexcusable!"

"Why would you be concerned about…." Steve began. Hugo interrupted.

"Because I am an FBI intern, sir."

Steve almost choked on a sip of coffee. He stared daggers at Robert.

"So Robert has an FBI agent for a roommate!" he exclaimed, still glaring at his withering son.

"He's not an agent Manning, Dad. He's a great guy!"

"Please, please. I'm sorry if I've caused embarrassment here. I was just hoping to correct any misconceptions about my profession…if that's possible."

"I don't have an argument with the organization per se, I just think they have a tendency to bully people."

"There are bullies in every profession, sir. Let me defend those who are not bullies. Our mission in the Federal Bureau of Investigation is to protect the people of the United States, simply said. Your mission in what you do at the state park, is to protect the wild life there. Mr. Ewing's mission is to protect the integrity of the personnel in the park. His son's job was to protect the lives of his men in combat, and against all enemies. We all have something to protect in our lives. Maybe that's the true mission in life.....to protect one another!"

Everyone at the dinner table sat with their mouths open. Doc stood and clapped.

"Well said, young man."

Steve grinned.

"How old are you Hugo?"

"Twenty-two, sir."

"Well, if the FBI doesn't work out for you, you should go into politics. I'd vote for you!"

Becky, Steve and Doc sat around the fireplace in the living room, while Robert, Hugo, Steven, Jr., and Jessica cleared the table and washed the dishes.

"That was some speech that boy gave a while ago." Doc observed. Everyone nodded.

"I think he's going into the wrong profession." Steve contributed. "and what about you, Doc?" Steve inquired, "you seem to have a lot on your mind these days."

There was no immediate answer, and Steve continued. "Jon is doing well according to what you have told us, so I would assume something else is bothering you."

Doc stood and stretched.

"Don't worry about it..... I think it's bed time for me, so I'll be going. Thank you so much you, guys. Thanksgiving is no time to be alone."

As he was going out the door, he turned to Steve and Becky.

"Some day I'll get all this off my chest, . See you tomorrow, Steve"

Mars

11/ 27 /'03

"We caught one! I fashioned a wire trap and set the bait. It worked.

It's not exactly conformed like a cockroach. It's long, and reddish in color and has two claw-like front appendages. Of all things...it hisses.

Janet put it in a kettle of boiling water and in a matter of minutes we had ourselves a perfect Thanksgiving dinner.

Happy Thanksgiving....again everyone."

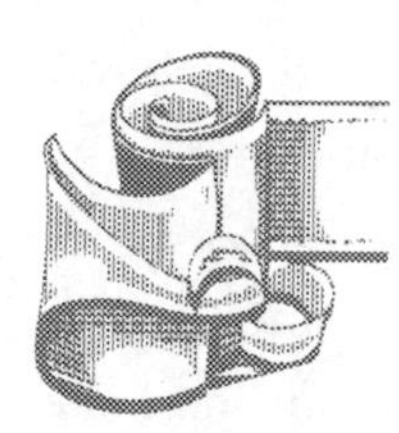

CHAPTER 15

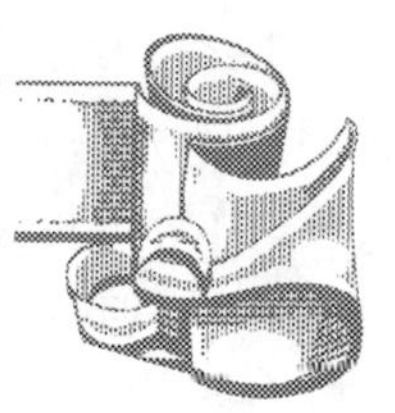

The Mehrabad International Airport lies within the boundaries of Tehran, Iran. It was where Uncle Jahangir and Farid arrived aboard flight 441 on Iran Air. The plane discharged atTerminal 2 gate. Jahangir and Farid walked, baggage in hand, to the front and hailed a cab.

"To Fajr Ashian," Uncle ordered. The cab pulled off.

"Where are we going?" Farid asked.

"You will see," was the answer with a smile.

The cab took the taxiway crossing over the Tehran Kervia Highway. A series of hangers and office buildings appeared. One building on the far side of the row of hangers bore a marquee which read: FAJR AEHIAN AIRCRAFT ENGINEERING AND MAINTENANCE CORPORATION.

"What is all this?" a skeptical Farid asked, "and when do I get to see my parents?"

"In due time, my nephew, in due time. First, I want you to see my most amazing project."

It was incredible what sat before Farid in the hanger closest to the engineering building. It was a fully fuseslaged aircraft sitting on a pierced-steel platform. It was bullet-like in shape, had swept back wings with large winglets on either side, a contoured cockpit windshield and four large jet exhausts in the rear. There were two round port holes on either side, and what looked to be an entrance on the pilot side. As Farid could remember, it was about the same volume in size as the Altair.

"How long have you people been working on this?" Farid asked.

"Long enough to get this far with everything but the computer input.....and that's just what we brought over with us."

"Then what am I doing here?"

"You, dear nephew, are my computer man. You will jack my computer laced jacket into our own main frame here, and then onto this magnificent aircraft."

"I could mess it up." Farid said with a sneer.

"You said you wanted to see your mother and father. It would be tragic to think of what would happen to them if*....you messed up."*

It suddenly came to Farid what this was all about. He and his family were being held hostage.

"Well, what shall it be?" asked the uncle.

After some hesitation, and though, Farid responded.

"Let's see the jacket."

Hugo Munoz and special agent Hal Holtz sat staring at the material on Holtz's desk. There were several computer chip casings and the dry-cleaning bag with the *Wallies Dry-Cleaning. Open 24hours* copy on it.

"What do you suppose all this means, Mr. Holtz?"

Holtz lit a cigarette and leaned back in his chair, still staring at the items on his desk.

"It might mean nothing. On the other hand, it might suggest that there was some work being done on a computer...maybe even that mainframe we found in the hanger last week. What the dry-cleaning bag means, I could't offer a guess."

"Obviously, someone in that group picked up their dry cleaning and changed into whatever piece of clothing was in the bag," Hugo offered," Where is this Wallies place?"

"Just about a block from here." Holtz answered. "I'm getting your drift. Maybe a little visit to our friend, Mr. Wallie"

Upon the showing of the FBI badge, the proprietor of Wallies allowed a search of the dry-cleaning registration book. There was no recognizable name, but after further questioning, Wallies owner recalled an event some weeks ago.

"This guy comes in with a sports jacket and a strange piece of material. Since we do alterations, he asked to have this piece of material sewed into the inside back of the jacket. The material had a weird texture, and when I asked him what it was, he was very vague, but was very precise about how it was to go on. The rough side was to face out, with the two tabs on the bottom."

"What did these tabs look like?" Holtz asked.

"They looked more like small plugs."

"Can you describe the guy?" Hugo inquired.

"Yeah... He was kind of dumpy...had a big nose and a beard, spoke very poor English, like some kind of arab."

"Anything else you can remember?"

"He wanted a rush job on it. I told him two weeks, but that wasn't good enough, so I cut it down to ten days...the best I could do."

Holtz handed the proprietor his card.

"Thank you very much for your help, sir. If you can remember anything else, call us at this number."

Wallies' owner brightened.

"One other thing. This may not be important, but when I asked him one more time what this pad was for, he said that he had a bad back and this pad was literally a portable heating pad."

"Based on my roommate's description of Uncle Jahangir, it was definitely him." Hugo relayed, "and Robert said the guy was clever as hell."

"So now, we have to assume that uncle and nephew have flown the coop with a dangerous amount of intelligence. Enough to endanger the security of the whole world."

"What do we do?" Hugo asked.

"I'm going to be making some phone calls. Tell your roommate that regardless of how he or his father feel about all this, they're now involved, and to be prepared to do some extensive traveling."

"Steve, come on up to my office for a few minutes will you?" Doc asked on his cell phone.

It had been raining most of the day so Steve drove his truck up to the headquarters building instead of the usual walk.

"Come on in, Steve, have a seat." Doc said cordially, "First of all, I want to thank you and Becky for that marvelous dinner last Thursday. She's quite a cook."

"I made the mash-potatoes and the dressing!" Steve offered with mild deference.

Doc laughed,

"Yeah, even they were good. You'll make a great couple. Just remember when your looking for someone to share a good meal with, I'm available." They both laughed.

Doc rose and walked over to the coffee pot...poured two cups and returned.

" I want to apologize for my short response to your question about my state of mind. I promised then that sometime in the future, I would discuss it. Well, now's the time."

Doc proceeded to relate his experience with Jon, and especially Crista Braun in Frankfurt the past September.

"Steve, it's the first time since Nancy's death many, many years ago, that I have met a women that evoked my passion for love as Nancy did. I know, maybe I should have recovered from the shock of losing her a long time ago, but I didn't."

Steve nodded his head in understanding.

Doc continued, "I've written Crista several letters..... hell, one a week since I've been back, but she hasn't responded to a one."

Steve sipped his coffee, looking over the lip of the cup at Doc, and trying to compose a suitable response.

"You say she lost both her husband and son?" Doc Nodded. Steve continued.

"Did it ever occur to you that she was going through the very same thing you were? Suddenly, she meets a guy that turns on the juices again, and she doesn't know how to handle it."

"But,..Steve, why doesn't she at least answer one of my letters?"

"I can't answer that, Doc, but I have a suggestion."

"What would that be?"

"Take some time off and go over there. If she's afraid to commit her emotions to an unknown quantity, your appearance will show her that your love is the real thing."

Doc brightened up.

"Hell of an idea!"

He rose from the desk, tossed his empty styrofoam coffee cup into the wastebasket.

"Right after your wedding, I'll take off. Then you can be *my* best man!"

"Deal!"

They shook hands.

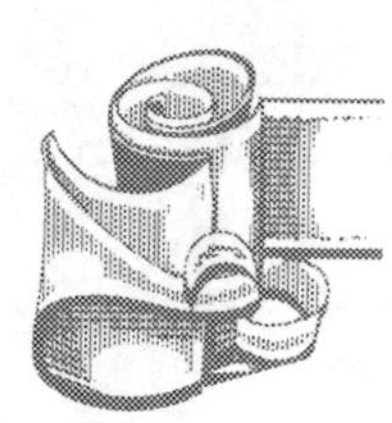

CHAPTER 16

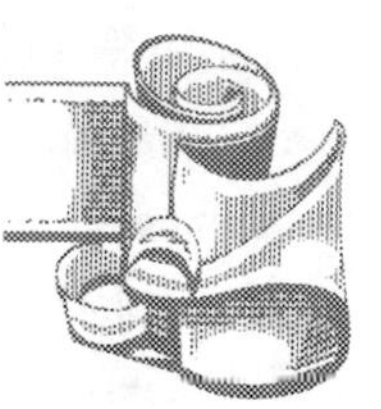

The wedding rehearsal took place the evening of December 14 in the Williams Creek United Methodist Church. The whole family was present, and went through the paces without a hitch.

"That scares the hell out of me", Steve said, "They say a bad rehearsal means a great performance. I wonder if the reverse is true."

"If I don't drop the ring, everything will work out fine." Doc spoke glibly.

Steve turned to Robert.

"I'm sorry Hugo could't make it."

"He had to go to DC with Agent Holtz. He expresses his regrets."

No one noticed the blush on Robert's face.

A light rehearsal dinner was given at the church, and everyone went their way in anticipation of the wedding the next afternoon..

December 15, 2003, 1p.m.

The wedding party included: Bride-Becky, Groom-Steve, Best man-Doc, Maid of Honor-Jessica, Ushers-Steven, Jr. & Robert. Only the front several rows in the church were occupied, mostly on Steve's side of the aisle. To the organ tune of Jeremiah Clarke's "The King's March", Becky walked down the aisle, escorted by Steven, Jr.

Both Bride and Groom glowed.

"Dearly beloved........."

Doc did not drop the ring.

Steve and Becky delayed their honeymoon so that Doc could travel overseas. He departed Indianapolis International on December 18 on Delta Flight 960 bound for Washington DC with one stop in Atlanta. He arrived at Reagan International at 10 a.m. and went directly to Walter Reed Hospital to visit Jon. He was amazed and pleased with his son' progress.

After a lengthy review of events at home, Doc relayed is true mission for going to Frankfurt.

"Dad, Steve has the right idea. If Crista still won't give you an answer, by God, drag her by the hair into your cave. She's yours...and my mother to be. So, go get her!"

With this ringing in Doc's ear, he continued his journey to Frankfurt.

A shock rang around the world when the headlines broke with:

RUSSIANS SEND MANNED
MISSION TO MARS.

Scientists the world over could not believe the Russians guile. The motive was obvious. They had to prove their scientific prowess. If the big story of late was the 'Mars Man', then they had to do it one better.

There were six crew members. A cosmonaut, a physician, and two married couples. They were to land on Mars, not planning to return. They also, most likely, were to search for the 'Mars Man'.

Incredibly insane was the scientific consensus. Unless the Russians had advanced beyond belief in the technology of space travel, they had just sent six people to their deaths for political reasons only.

Doc's flight landed in Frankfurt in the late afternoon, and after clearing through customs, he went directly to the Frankfurt Hospital.

"I'm sorry, Mr. Ewing, Nurse Braun is no longer here."

"No longer here? Where is she?"

"One moment, please." The nurse at the reception desk disappeared, and shortly, an elderly nurse that Doc recognized, appeared.

"Hello again Herr Ewing. Please have a seat with me."

They sat and the elderly nurse introduced herself.

"I am Greta Schmitt. You and I never met officially while you and your son were here, but I know you through nurse Braun."

Doc was uncomfortable in his anticipation of what this conversation was leading to.

"I came to see her....."

"Crista has gone to Bremen to seek a new life for herself."

"A new life? What do you mean?" Doc asked.

"You will find her at the Bremen Monastery."

"Monastery?" Doc almost shouted, "I don't understand!"

"As Crista has told you, she has lived a life of loneliness and despair ever since the death of her husband and child many years ago. She at first chose nursing as a means of escape. Until she met you, Herr Ewing, that was satisfactory. But when you proposed to her.....yes, she confided in me. When you proposed to her, she became confused, and her despair returned to the point where she realized that there had to be another more permanent escape."

"But a monastery is for...."

"Nuns, Herr Ewing. That is what she has decided to do."

"A nun?" Doc was on the verge of tears.

"As I understand the procedure, she is consider a novice now...not a full fledged nun. But, Herr Ewing, I would think twice before going to see her at this stage of the transition. I know Crista very well. She is a highly sensitive, loving person. Seeing you again might destroy her."

"You say she confided in you. Did she tell you how she felt about me?"

"She very clearly fell in love with you as you did her. Please, for her sake, and yes, for yours too, leave it at that."

There was heavy silence as a jumble of muddled thoughts ran through Doc's head. He massaged the tears away from his eyes and smiled.

"Thank you, nurse..."

"Nurse Schmitt," She returned the smile, " You are very welcome. I only wish it was better news for you....and for Crista."

Doc rose. He chuckled, as they shook hands.

"Pardon the sudden levity, but I was thinking of a discussion that a young man and I had during the past Thanksgiving. He made the observation that we were all born to protect one another.

"Quite a profound young man." She bowed, "Have a safe trip home, Herr Ewing."

The sun was setting as Doc left the hospital. It had been snowing and with the sound of carolers down the street, it presented a perfect old world Christmas setting.

It was dark now and Doc had lost track of the miles he had walked. He suddenly realized that he had made no hotel accommodations His first effort was successful, and he wearily entered his room. He hadn't eaten since noon, but he wasn't hungry. He tossed his luggage into a corner and fell across the bed. He lay there for some time staring at the ceiling thinking...thinking...thinking. Then he threw his arm across his face and wept softly before slipping into a deep sleep.

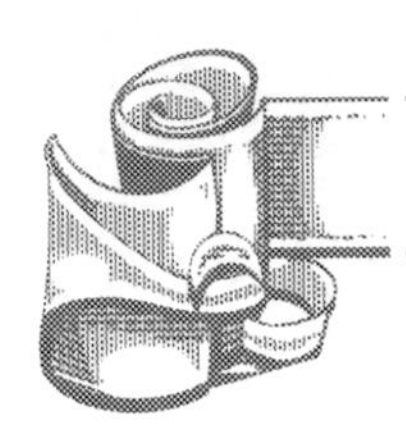

CHAPTER 17

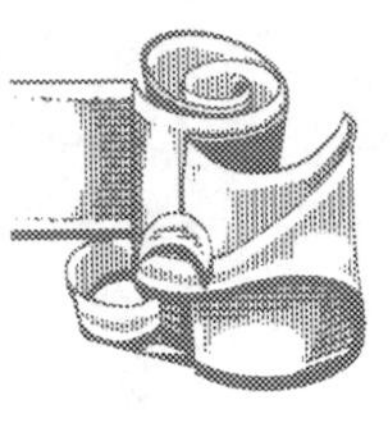

Mars

12/23/'03

"I suppose all of you there on earth are getting ready for the big day. I wonder in the distant past...and I mean the distant past... if whatever life form there might have been here, saw a star in the east, and long before us, celebrated the coming of a great king like we do now. I have a theory about all that.I think billions of years ago, Mars was like earth. It had a population. They might even have looked like us, but that's not important. They had intelligence, and they developed technologically, like we are doing now. They might even have done some space traveling.

The environment began to change as their industry threw more and more carbon dioxide into the air. The population here ignored the signs as weather became more violent, and temperatures rose, causing areas of land to be submerged by rising waters. They all attributed this to cyclic phenomena. Over time, lakes and rivers began to dry up. Where we are now located, there are signs that water once flowed on the surface of Mars.Water became scarce, and once upon a time when wars were fought over oil and land and plain old ego, it was now over precious water. What we, in many places on earth, take for granted.

Life became a living hell here. Whole civilizations began dying off. Wars, famine, and pestilence ran rampant. Soon, all life vanished…except maybe a few mutated cockroaches. Nature took over completely.One hundred plus mile per hour winds blew all the topsoil away. Nothing could grow. Geomagnetic sun storms stripped Mars of a greater part of its gravity, and thinned the breathable atmosphere, so that what was left is the Mars we see today. A barren, dry planet….which, regardless of scientist's wishful thinking, in my opinion, can never be restored to accommodate our population.

So there's my Christmas message, to whoever gives a damn.

The Eastern Star may have shown here once, but as it turns out, they never understood the message.

Merry Christmas one and all."

It was early Christmas Eve. Steve and Doc sat in the headquarters office preparing to close it up for the week-end.

"Are you sure you won't spend Christmas Eve with us, Doc?"

Doc poured eggnog from a cardboard container into two cups. He lifted his toward Steve.

"Thanks anyway, Steve. I'd only be a drag. There's not one hell of a lot for me to celebrate these days. Here's to you and yours." They downed the eggnog.

A car door slammed outside. The front door of the building opened and a familiar figure stood at the entrance to Doc's office.

"I think I have a little brandy to add to that eggnog."

It was Jon.... One hand with a brandy bottle, The other, a cane.

Both Steve and Doc jumped to their feet.

"I'll be a son-of-a bitch!" Doc screamed, "How...."

"I guess when you have the Medal of Honor, you can get away with most anything," Jon jested, "Anyway, I got a ten-day leave, and I think it's time to add the brandy to that eggnog., Merry Christmas!"

They added the brandy and drank.

"Hey, Steve," Doc chirped. "If that invitation is still open, we'll both be there."

They were both there and having a most merry time. Steven, Jr., had brought Jessica and took the occasion to announce their engagement. More eggnog and brandy.

Robert was there in body, but was unusually sedate.

"How is the leg?" Steve asked Jon.

"A little sore yet, but I'm quite a bit ahead of schedule on it. When I get back, they'll put the finishing touches on it, I'll be the best kickball artist on the block." They all laughed. No more eggnog....just brandy.

They gathered around the piano to Jessica's playing and sang carols at the top of their voices, including the sobering " White Christmas."

As they sang, and without notice, Doc walked to the living room window to hide the tears in his eyes.

I wonder what she's doing now, he thought.

The holy services were over, and Crista retired to her room and sat down to write a letter:

My dearest Doc,

I've never gotten used to that name—Doc. But it's you and I'm now more than used to it...I dream about it.

Does that surprise you? Nurse Schmitt told me of your visit last week and although I was greatly grieved that you didn't come to Bremen, I agree with her advice not to.

I apologize for not answering any of your letters, but quite frankly I didn't know what to say. I made a decision to go elsewhere and try to find some kind of peace. It's marvelous here. The nuns and Mother Superior are very kind to me, but, Doc dear, I can't get you out of my mind.

You proposed to me months ago and I simply didn't know how to respond. I should have said ...yes., but I didn't. Now I'm wondering if you still want me after all this. I would gladly come to America and start a new life with you.

Please tell me it's not too late.

My love forever and ever,
Crista

She leaned back in her chair and reread what she had written. Then balled it up and tossed it in the wastebasket.

No one went home the night before so the house was full of make shift sleeping arrangements. Brandy made for good sleeping, so it wasn't until 8:30 a.m. that Steve joined Becky in the kitchen preparing breakfast for eight.

"Glad I bought extra eggs." he said, as he kissed the back of her neck.

"'Could have used more bread, but what we have will do. " she answered returning the kiss, "Merry Christmas."

"Same to you." Steve placed the dishes on the table as a token of staying out of the way.

"I wonder what's bugging Robert?" Steve asked, "He was droopy all last night...not himself."

"Why don't you ask him? I think I hear him rustling around in his room."

"You....we, what!?" Steve all but screamed.

Robert, in a humble voice,

"We have to fly to Washington DC this Wednesday."

"What the hell for?"

"Special agents Holtz and Broyles, Hugo, you and I have to appear before a special cabinet review board, which will include the President of the United States., heads of the FBI and CIA, and the military chiefs of staff." Robert squeaked.

Steve turned white in spite of his brandy coloring.

"What the hell have you gotten us into now, Robert, and what the hell have I been telling you about those creepy guys?"

"Dad, please settle down and listen. It looks like my former roommate, Farid, and his uncle have taken all they need back to Iran to build another Altair. If that's the case, and if they're successful, nothing in the free world can stop them from ruling the sky.... and land for that matter. They need our input."

Steve had to sit and digest what Robert had just said.

"Why do they need me?"

"I guess it's because you were involved with Gerald Pence and The Altair....and.... because you married his daughter."

The Christmas day laze had set in at the Gordon household. All except Steve who was in another room trying to reach special agent Broyles by phone. Steven, Jr., and Jessica had gone for a walk to enjoy the afternoon sun.

Jon and Doc had gone to the park.

Becky was in the kitchen preparing for the Christmas dinner.

Robert approached her.

"Dad's pretty ticked I guess," he mumbled over her shoulder.

"You gave him quite a jolt this morning, Robert," she responded.

"He threatened to wring my neck,"

... a pause... "would he really do that?"

Becky slipped the twice baked potatoes into the oven and turned.

"Yes!"

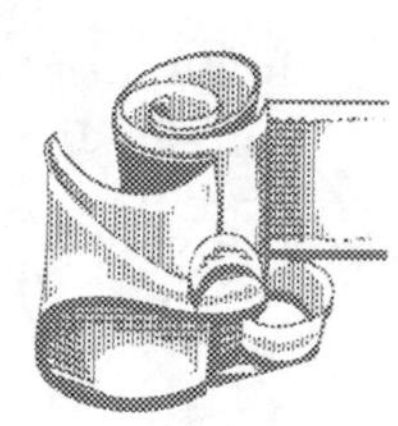

CHAPTER 18

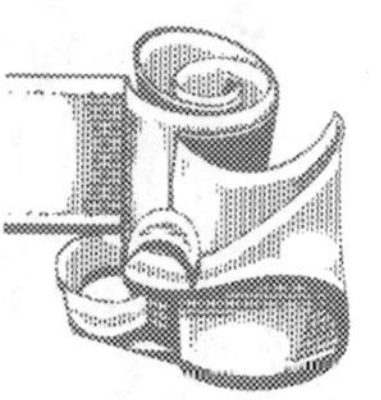

Crista's novice roommate was assigned the house cleaning chores in their room. Crista was elsewhere doing her Christmas Day chores.

She picked up the wastebasket and noticed the balled up letter that Crista had tossed there the night before. It was taken out and placed on the table.

Curiosity reigned supreme and after minutes of resisting temptation, the roommate set her broom against the wall and read the letter.

"Mother Agatha, I know I have sinned, but I really feel you should be aware of this." She handed the crinkled letter to the Mother Superior. She motioned for the roommate to sit while she read it. She pressed it against her chest when she finished. She spent several moments deep in thought.

"You were right in bringing this to me, Anna. Thank you."

After the roommate left, Mother Superior Agatha summoned Sister Beatrice.

" Find Crista and tell her I wish to speak with her immediately."

The Russians reported to the world that their manned Mars mission was proceeding as expected, and all was well.

"They would have said that if the thing had blown up on the pad." the professor observed. Those Russians!

Steve finally reached agent Broyles at his home.

"To what do I owe this call on a holy day?" he asked.

Steve was hostile.

"I'll give you three guesses! What the hell is this about my son and me going to Washington?"

"What has he told you?"

"Enough to establish the fact that it's bullshit!"

"I gather from your tone of voice that you don't like the idea."

"Bingo! Your perceptive abilities are remarkable. What if we refused to go?"

There was silence and a deep breath.

"Look at it this way, Mr. Gordon. You get an all expenses paid trip to the nation's capital, stay in a first class hotel, get to meet the President of The United States, and practically the whole damn administration. Most people would kill for that opportunity."

"I would kill, but not for that. I repeat...what if I refuse?"

"Call it a subpoena, a warrant. We have legal ways of persuading you, Mr. Gordon."

"Dammit! It's guys like you that turn me against dark glasses. What arrangements are being made?"

"Agent Holtz and our intern are already there setting the whole thing up. We will pick you and your son up by helicopter on Wednesday morning at precisely 10 a.m.... in front of the Williams Creek State Park Headquarters Building. From there we go to Indianapolis, and depart from the airport on an Air Force jet.Thank you for your cooperation, Mr. Gordon."

So went the remainder of Christmas Day, and to his relief, Robert survived.

Mars

12/ 26/ '03

"Just a short message today. We managed to clear the mouth of the cave of the dust storm debris, which allowed the extreme cold to enter. We spend most of the time inside the Altair as a result.

I understand the Russians have sent a party up to join us. I wish them well, but don't have much faith in their ability to get here in one piece. In any case, we'll be looking for them.

I am concerned about another thing. The first string computer has been acting erratically of late. I tried the second and third back-ups and get the same thing. I'd hate to think what would happen if they gave out on us.

Will keep you posted."

The professor shook his head. If the Russians arrive safely could they be their saviors?

The University of Arizona Observatory expressed their concern also.

Yes, the accommodations were first class. Robert and Steve enjoyed a delicious room service meal, and spent the evening watching a TV movie until the phone rang.

"Holtz here. We're to begin the hearing at 10.a.m. in the capital building conference room. We'll be by to pick you two up at 9:30 sharp. Any questions?"

"Yes, do we pay the gratuity here or do you?"

Steve had not lost his sense of humor.

There was major disappointment. The President was represented by the Chairman of the Armed Service committee; The Chiefs of Staff were represented by a Rear Admiral, and an Army Colonel. The FBI and CIA offered two third tier flunkies that were probably interns like Hugo.

As they were sitting, Steve whispered to Broyles.

"Boy, did you over sell!"

There was no comment from the Indianapolis agent.

Robert waved to Hugo.

"Hi there, roomy." Both Steve and Hugo felt that this added nicely to what was shaping up to be a masterful fiasco.

Agent Holtz rose and did the introductions. He then moved to the podium at the head of the table. He began with what was probably going to be the most interesting bit of information of the whole meeting.

"We have cause to believe that Farid Scherzi and his parents have been abducted by Iranian personnel, and have become part of a scheme by the Iranian government to build a state of the art aircraft in what we shall call the Altair Class. We are quite sure where they are, and where the area of the construction is located. It is the opinion of our government, and several personnel here, that should such an aircraft be successfully built with the same capabilities of the so called Altair, it would jeopardize the security of all free world countries. In short, we have nothing to equal it."

"Where is the Altair?" a misinformed department representative asked. There was an embarrassed hush, as Holtz shuffled some papers around at the podium.

"The Altair is, at the moment, indisposed." was his response

The Colonel spoke up," Why don't we bomb the hell out of them?"

Another hushed moment.

"That would endanger Farid and his parents."

There were no further comments. Holtz pointed to Steve.

"Mr Gordon, could you relay your experiences with this situation?"

Steve didn't bother to stand.

"I had nothing to do with the building of this aircraft. I managed to save Mr Pence from his kidnappers, who were apparently after the plans.... including an agent of the FBI."

Both FBI agents present dropped their heads.

"Other than that, I had no further involvement."

"Did you not marry his daughter?" The Admiral asked.

"With all due respect, sir, what the hell does that have to do with world security?" The Admiral shuffled some papers..

Holtz pointed to Robert.

"You were part of the so called Raisbeck Engineering Group at Purdue University that developed the fuselage for the Altair."

Robert cleared his throat as he stood up.

"Yes, sir, but that was my whole involvement other than spending time at the lab watching it being constructed. We didn't even know at the time what we were developing this fuselage for. I came on line late in this whole thing, so that's all I can tell you."

"What can you tell us about this Iranian, Farid?"

"Nothing, except Mr. Pence gave him the books containing the plans and formulas for safekeeping."

"Where were these books kept?

"In our lab at the Aeronautics Building at Purdue."

"In your opinion, Mr. Gordon, could this young man, Farid, build another Altair?"

"He is very bright, sir, but I don't think that, on his own, he could have overcome all the obstacles, although he thought he could."

"Thank you, Mr Gordon."

Steve was pleased with Robert's performance and nodded his head toward him as he sat down.

"Mr. Munoz, do you have anything to say?"

Hugo rose from his seat, and walked to the podium almost shoving Holtz out of the way.

"Yes, I sure do. What hasn't been mentioned here is that this whole thing could be a hoax! Who knows where Pence really is? He says that he's on Mars. If the Russians get there in one piece and prove that he is, I'll be a buyer. Otherwise...forget it."

Holtz gathered his papers.

"Gentlemen, I introduce our CIA representative, Mr. Ralph Johnson."

Some one in the group began an applause, but backed off with a sheepish smile.

"All I have to say is that until proven otherwise, we will consider this a top priority program. We will assume that Iran has the capability of building this thing. How far along they are at this point we cannot guess. We also feel a responsibility for the welfare of three US citizens. We have people in Iran who can keep us appraised of the situation, and when it is time, to act unilaterally if necessary. Thank you."

Good God, thought Steve. That was it? A two day waste of tax payer money to hear several low level bureaucrats thump their chests? Well any way, the government paid the gratuity.

They flew home that afternoon.

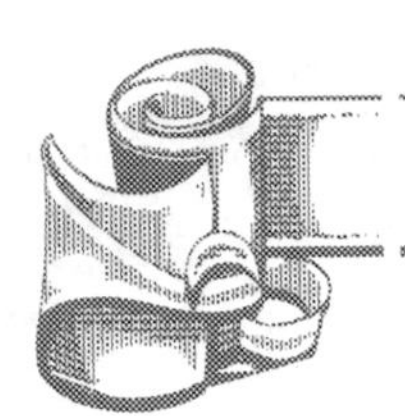

CHAPTER 19

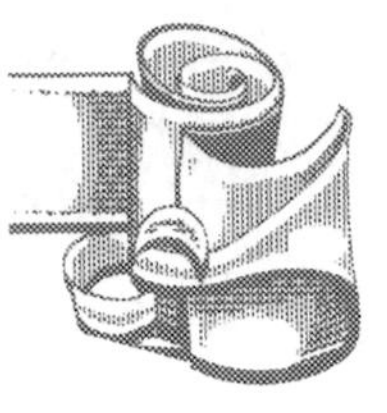

"Please sit down, Crista."

Crista sat at Reverend Mother Agatha's desk across from her. Mother Agatha opened a drawer and withdrew the wrinkled letter. She gently passed it across the desk to Crista.

"I'm sure you are familiar with this." she said kindly. Crista flushed and dropped her head.

"It was a horrid moment of weakness, Superior Mother."

"No, my dear, it was a moment of true love." Mother Agatha pulled the letter back and studied it.

"This man....Doc, must be a wonderful person to generate such feeling from a woman such as you."

Crista perked up.

"He is, Mother Agatha. But.... he represents those earthly things that I have agreed to ....." Mother Agatha raised her hand to hush her.

"My dear, years ago you suffered a grievous loss in the tragic death of your husband and young son. Your amazing capacity for love had nowhere to go then, so you chose to become a nurse. That way, you were able to help others in pain. Then Doc came along and your earthly longing for love was reborn. He proposed and you weren't able to handle the sudden surge of that love. So, you came here to put that feeling in a higher direction."

Mother Agatha put her left hand up.

"This ring signifies my love for our Savior Jesus Christ… an ethereal love that fulfills *my* life. God has given you the means of fulfilling that capacity of love in your heart. By all means, take it."

Tears welled up in Crista's eyes as she felt both a sense of relief and guilt.

"But Mother Superior, you are a woman of God… above temptations and…." Again Crista was hushed by Agatha's burst of laughter.

"Listen to me, child. There once was a young girl who had just taken her final vows. She was only twenty-four years of age then. It was the year 1964. She was sent to America for a conference at the University of Notre Dame. Lodging was scarce because of the conference, so they put her group in the Notre Dame Stadium dorms. It so happens that Notre Dame was scheduled to open the season against Wisconsin that Saturday. This young nun was awed by the magnitude of it all. Late that evening on the Thursday before the game, she managed to wander into the Fighting Irish locker room. There was a bin of practice footballs. She took one and on an impulse, walked out onto the field. Of course the stadium was empty. In the far end, up high was the famous Touchdown Jesus. She could not resist the temptation, Crista. She tucked the football under her arm, lifted her habit and dashed toward the far end zone. She could hear the crowd screaming and the band playing....Cheer,Cheer for Old Notre Dame!

As she neared the five yard line, she lost her grip on her habit, tripped and fell. The ball bounced into the end zone and all was suddenly quiet again. She lay there dumbfounded. She could see the headlines—NUN JINXES FIGHTING IRISH FOR 1964 SEASON!"

Both Crista and Mother Agatha laughed .

"Crista, dear, that little nun was me, and believe-it-or-not, the Fighting Irish whipped Wisconsin handily that Saturday and went on to lose only one game the rest of the year. Please, never think that all earthly temptations are bad."

She slid the letter across to Crista.

"I want you to rewrite this letter word for word and send it. You deserve each other."

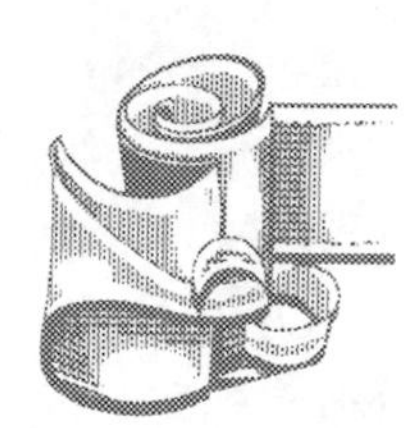

CHAPTER 20

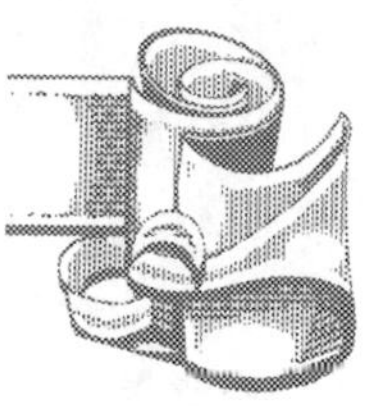

After several hours of closely supervised work on the main frame computer, Farid was allowed to visit his parents, lodged not far from the hanger.

"We were told that if we didn't accompany them back to Iran, they would kill you. We didn't know what or who to believe." Farid's father relayed.

While these words were being spoken, Farid drifted around the room searching for hidden microphones. He found one screwed into the bedside table lamp. Motioning his parents to follow him, he went into the bathroom and turned the shower, and sink faucets on. He searched the area quickly and was satisfied there were no 'bugs'. He spoke softly.

"Listen to me carefully. I will figure a way out of this. Be ready to move on a moment's notice. Cooperate with these people until then. I love you."

He was driven back to the hanger and more supervised work.

Updates on the progress of the Russian manned mission to Mars suddenly stopped. This led to much speculation on its fate. Most scientists the world over were ready to accept the worst. It was what most of them expected.

It was Steven, Jr.'s turn to monitor the screens at the Goethe Link Observatory. He was a charter member of the IU Astronomy Club and had become a favorite of Professor Emerson of the Astronomy Department. The downloaded Mars messages from the University of Arizona's Steward Observatory had dropped off to zero ever since the alarming report that the Altair's computers were acting up. It was acknowledged by the monitoring scientists that if indeed the computers broke down, there would be little or no chance of survival for Pence and his companion.

In any case, it was December 30....two days away from 2004. It had been Pence's habit to send messages on special occasions such as he did before Thanksgiving and Christmas. Now they were waiting for his New Year's message which, at this point, had not come.

There had been no word from the Russian mission either. It was the consensus that a failure would never be reported and if no update was made within a reasonable time, they could all assume the worst.

Steven had brought his books with him, but had no compulsion to study. His and Jessica's wedding had been planned for June 20, after her graduation. In the absence of any activity on the monitoring screen, that was on his mind.

They had decided that she would teach until Steven received his Master's Degree, and then go for *her* Master's.

No family was planned for the immediate future. Between him and Jessica, his father, Steve and Becky, a moderate family tree was beginning. But, what about Robert? So far it had been all adventure and fun...no romantic connections. Oh well, there always had to be the black sheep, and at this point, Robert was well qualified.

The phone rang.

"Doctor Dunbar here from the Steward Observatory. Heads up! We have a Mars messages coming in."

Steve's attention jumped to the screen.

Mars
12/28/'13

"Let me explain the workings of my computers. Through many hours of experimentation and of course, innovation, I was able to develop intelligence in computers, to the point that I can carry on conversations with them. Of course you know that the Altair is controlled by them and couldn't fly without them. There are three of them aboard....the main one and two back-ups. If the main one goes out, the second one takes over while the third one repairs number one computer. This is what occurred when we first landed here.

The point I'm trying to make in all this is that the reason the computer was acting strangely is that it was trying to tell me that there is an attempt somewhere on earth to duplicate the data it carries. I can only assume that it comes from the plans and formulas that I gave to the Iranian Farid Sherazi for safe keeping. Why? Call it super ego, but I couldn't let years of effort go down the drain. I never dreamt he'd try to replicate it. Fortunately, the computers can communicate with each other once he completes the duplication.

I've asked my main line to send a trial message to who ever is working the earth version to see what happens.

So, friends, my computers are all right...not to worry.

A Happy New Year to all.

P.S.- The years up here are equivalent to two on earth, so, Happy New Year twice!"

The rain pattered off of their umbrellas as Steve and Becky stood over Carolyn's grave. Both were silent. Becky looked up at Steve's face and could't tell if the drops falling down his cheek were rain or tears.

A roll of thunder echoed in the distance as Steve leaned over and placed a red carnation on the grave. It was Carolyn's favorite flower.

"There are not many wives who would tolerate this, you know," Steve said, straightening up, and putting his arm around Becky's waist.

"New Year's Eve would seem to be an appropriate time to celebrate a loved one's life." Becky slipped her arm into Steve's arm and drew him closer, "I want you to make this a tradition each year. That's what I would want if it were me lying there." He hugged her back.

"Thank you."

Doc and Jon were sitting in front of their fireplace staring blankly into the crackling flames and waiting out the old year when the phone rang. It was from the lodge desk.

"Doc, you have an airmail, special delivery letter here."

"Does it look like anything important?" Doc asked lazily.

"Hell, it's from a monastery in Bremen Germany! I'd say it's damn important.....excuse the language!"

Doc woke up,

"I'll be right up!"

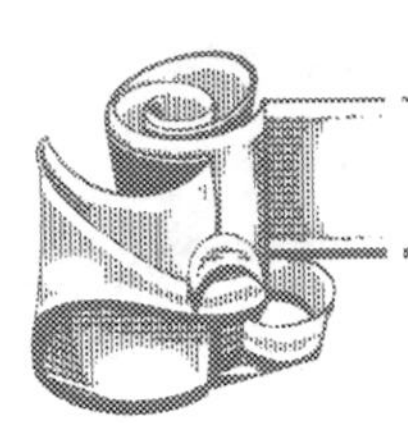

CHAPTER 21

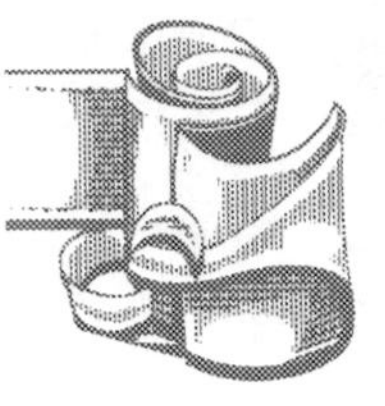

Farid sat in front of the onboard computer with his notebook on his lap. He had finished the transfer of data from his uncle's coat, and was entering the final coding when, to his surprise and shock, the computer began to flash a sentence across its screen.

"I am computer one aboard the Altair, which is presently on the planet Mars. I have been instructed to ask if you are Farid ?"

The screen went blank, and Farid still in a state of shock, whispered,

"Yes."

Understanding the delay in the transmission from earth to Mars, Farid waited nervously for a response. six and a half minutes went by and once again the screen jumped to life.

"Where are you, and what is the status of the craft?"

Farid assured himself that no one was close by to overhear his response. With as few words as possible, he relayed the situation to the computer and sat back to await the response. It came.

" Please stand by."

At that moment, Uncle Jahangir entered the aircraft.

"Well my nephew, how are you progressing with the transfer?"

Farid was momentarily startled by his entrance but hoped it wasn't noticeable.

"I should be able transfer your ID to the computer by day after tomorrow."

"Oh, such a delay! I had hoped by now...considering the length of time you've been working on it...it would be almost immediate. I'm sure your parents would think so too."

Two minutes had gone by. Farid nervously glanced at the blank screen.

"You brought me here to do a very complicated job. It would be helpful if you'd let me do it."

Uncle laughed,

"Testy are you, my nephew. Perhaps I should spend more time looking over your shoulder to assure that there is no hanky-panky."

Perspiration dampened Farid's forehead.

Four minutes had expired.

"You do what you think you have to. Also, I'd appreciate it if you'd stop calling me 'nephew'. I'm no more your nephew than I am a bucket of rocks!"

Jahangir's joyful expression soured.

"You are very insolent, young man. I would watch your manners." Jahangir said over his shoulder as he moved toward the exit.

The computer screen came on.

"Not now!" Farid screamed. Jahangir turned.

"What's that you said?"

A trickles of perspiration stung Farid's eyes.

"I was just testing!"

Jahangir left the aircraft shaking his head. Farid breathed a sigh of relief and leaned toward the computer screen.

"Now, now!"

"Here is what you must do. Put your hand on the screen so that it can read you as the operator of the aircraft.When the time comes...pretend to register Jahangir as the pilot. It will not take. Then when you make your move, the aircraft will be at your disposal."

Farid did as instructed and then leaned back dabbing his forehead with his shirt sleeve. Things were beginning to fall in place.

Blake Domian was the CIA agent out of Chicago. He was circled by special FBI agents Hal Holtz, and Kyles Broyles, intern Hugo Munoz and Professor Emerson, around the computer at the Goethe Link Observatory. It was a conference call sponsored by the CIA and also involving agents from the CIA headquarters in Fairfax, Virginia, FBI headquarters personnel in Washington>D.C., and several high ranking military representatives.

Mars

01/03/'04

> *"This transmission is directional. Only those effected by it will receive it. I appreciate the participation of all you people, even though I know there are many that doubt my veracity.*

Never-the-less, I must report that I am in contact with Iranian Farid Sherazi who, along with his parents, are being held hostage by Iranian personnel out side of Tehran.The message says that the Iranians have moved faster on the development of the Altair replica than we thought possible.We must not allow this to become operational.

Between the computers aboard the Altair here and their aircraft, they have devised a means of setting up a rescue plan. We must, however, have the support of both the Division Special Activities of the CIA, or the Air Force Special Forces. Farid's primary, concern is the safety of his parents who are being held a short distance from the hanger where this craft is being assembled.

Farid now has control of the Altair Class aircraft, and can use it to support the escape plan. He knows that he must get his parents into the construction area and aboard the ship before the plan can proceed. However, we will need a covert distraction from one of the units mentioned above as part of the operation. I would suggest a SAD attack, but, I'm no military man, so it's up to you experts.

For you doubters, please assume that what I say is fact and act accordingly."

Hugo, the strongest doubter in the Goethe Link group, shook his head.

"Maybe the guy is really up there."

The only excitement on New Years Eve was Doc's letter from Bremen. Steve, Becky and Robert spent a quiet evening at home, and Steven celebrated the coming of the New Year with Jessica and her family.

Doc made a call to the monastery to tell them of his intent to travel there immediately. He and Jon began packing in preparations for their trip east the following day. The coming year promised much to celebrate for them both.

Steve, Becky and Robert had fallen asleep before midnight and only the sound of fireworks in the distance aroused them to the entrance of 2004. A quick toast followed, and then back to bed. So much for *their* New Year's celebration.

Doc arrived in Bremen the evening of New Years day and went straight to the monastery. He stood before the entrance and waited for Mother Agatha to summons Crista.

Jon had agreed to cut his leave short and return to Walter Reed Hospital for the remainder of his rehabilitation. The flight to Amsterdam thence to Bremen seemed to take forever to Doc, but now he was here standing nervously waiting for the woman he loved. She appeared dressed in street clothes and holding a small suitcase. She was radiant, he thought.

After a short prayer by Mother Agatha, they said their farewells.

"God bless you both." she called out as they descended the steps of the monastery and out onto the streets of Bremen to a waiting taxi.

"Would you mind terribly if I pay one final visit to the cemetery?" Crista asked.

"Of course not." Doc answered.

The taxi took them to the Frankfurt Cemetery. The taxi waited while they took the short walk to the graves of her husband, Max Braun, and son, Jacob Braun. Crista bowed her head in reverence..." Dearest son and husband, I am going on a new journey to a new life, but I will always carry with me the memories of the love and devotion we gave each other." She lifted her head and linked arms with Doc.

"Now, let's go home."

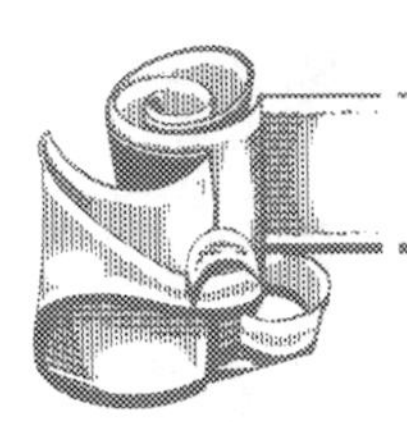

CHAPTER 22

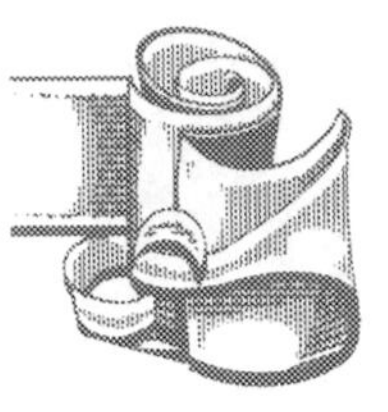

Farid sat in the aircraft watching Jahangir come through the side door of the hanger. In the plane with Farid was a co-worker who appeared to be following a final check list. He too watched Jahangir as he approached the plane. Quickly, the co-worker leaned over Farid's shoulder, and whispered,

"You must get your parents into the aircraft soon. At seventeen hundred hours today, all hell will break loose. A CIA Special Activities Unit will attack the hanger area to distract the Iranians, while you move out with this craft.Timing is of utmost importance. Good luck." He went back to his check list with an air of nonchalance as Jahangir entered.

"I look forward to tomorrow, my ex-nephew," he said with a wry grin, "I'm assuming we are on schedule for the ID transfer."

Farid feigned a confident attitude.

"We are, my ex-uncle. Allow me a request."

Jahangir ignored the co-worker who left the aircraft.

"And what would that be?"

"My parents have never seen this.... What have you called it." waving his arm around the cabin.

"The Aryan...ruler of the sky!" Jahangir announced proudly, "and why do your parents need to see it?"

"I'd like them to see this beautiful ship and your genius."

"Nonsense!" the ex-uncle shook his head, and as he was moving toward the exit he paused in thought and turned.

"All right. I see no danger in letting them see my genius. I will send the limousine for them tonight."

"Sir, they retire very early in the evening. Could you, just this once, indulge their routine?"

"Very well. I will send for them now." Jahangir said and left.

Farid leaned back in disbelief. By God, what luck!

Robert returned to the Purdue campus on Monday morning, January 5 to find Hugo, sitting at his desk in a high state of anxiety.

"What are you all buzzed up about?" Robert jibed, tossing his duffel bag on his bed.

"I hope I have the right to be! I'm waiting for a call on my cell phone, and...." He had hardly gotten his answer out when his cell phone buzzed. He turned it on, listened and buttoned off, face beaming.

"This is the kind of thing that makes my job such a whiz."

He set about explaining the whole Farid situation to Robert. The further he went, the brighter Robert's face became.

"You mean it's coming off at this moment?" Robert asked.

"It's ten after eight here....ten after five in Tehran, and if everything is on schedule...yes, it's happening at this moment!"

At ten minutes to five, Fahangir entered the aircraft to find, to his dismay, Farid and his parents. His face flushed with anger.

"I don't believe I gave you permission to bring your parents *aboard* this plane!" He blared.

"You didn't say they couldn't." Farid countered.

"I want them out this minute!"

Farid stood up and leaned over the smaller man.

"I'm afraid not, my dear, dear ex-uncle!" Farid threw a fist across Fahangir's jaw just as the sound of a heavy helicopter and gun fire echoed through the hanger.

Fahangir was staggered, but not hurt. He was able to draw a pistol when the sound of the chaos distracted him. Farid knocked the weapon from his hand, followed by a savage knee to the groin. Fahangir fell and writhed in pain on the cabin floor.

Farid placed his hand on the computer screen and screamed, "Blast the hanger door down and let's get the hell out of here!"

A laser bolt collapsed the door and with a hum of the engines, the ship moved toward it.

Farid collared the fallen Fahangir and dragged him to the exit door. Sliding it open, he shoved him out.

"Farewell, my.... ex-whatever!" Farid yelled above the tumult and slid the hatch shut as the craft cleared the hanger and shot up into the sky.

The onboard computer was now under the complete command of Farid who gave the order....

"Attack!"

The aircraft swept down the length of the airport runway knocking out a squadron of Iranian commandos charging toward the beleaguered hanger and at the same time blasting two Iranian jet fighters taxing to take off.

Farid screamed in delight.

"Go get 'em, you wonderful machine! I now recommission you,"the Orion!"

The SAD Unit, suffering only one minor casualty, boarded their helicopter and lifted off. The Orion swung around and over the helicopter as it rose and, on Farid's command, deployed it's protective shield over both craft. This rendered the Iranian ground fire ineffectual. Mission completed.

"Mom and Pop, let's escort these braves boys home!"

Robert sat back in amazement.

"When will you know how it went?" He asked eagerly.

"Our contact in Tehran will message the CIA headquarters and they will inform our group here. But, I'm betting on a huge success."

Robert turned around to his books, opened his chemistry text and pretended he was studying. Then he turned back to Hugo.

"I wonder if the FBI could use someone with an aeronautical engineering degree?"

"What would your dad think?" Hugo said with a grin.

Robert paused and then turned back to his chemistry book.

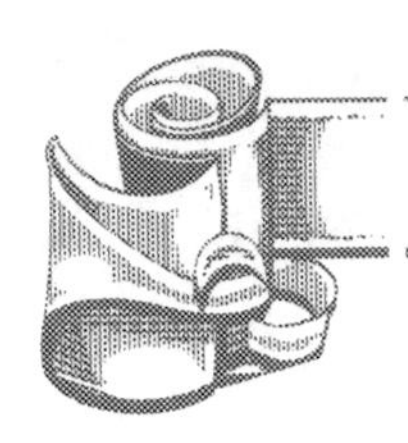

CHAPTER 23

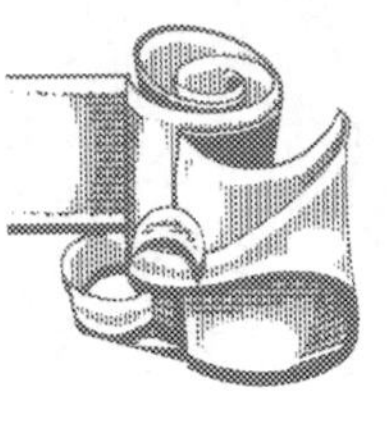

Mars
01/05/'04

Our onboard computer tells us that things went well in Tehran. It's amazing what the modern day computer has come to. As my computer is relating, the aircraft, which Farid is now calling Orion, has crossed the Iranian border into Iraq escorting the SAD helicopter.This may lead to some complications when the USA military there attempts to take possession of the craft. Between the two computers, this will not be allowed, no matter how Farid handles it.

But to more urgent affairs. Janet is due at any moment. I'm not sure how to deliver babies, but I've seen movies on how it's done....hot water, towels, clean hands, and a lot of panic. I'm hoping my computer will help.Whenever it happens, it will be the first child born on Mars. Not many people will be able to say that... for awhile anyway."

The SAD helicopter put down at the Bagdad airport, but after one final salute pass over the field, the Orion made it clear it had no intention of landing. Two F-22s had come up and now flew on either side of it with other thoughts in mind.

"This is Captain Raymond Carothers, United States Air Force. It is our desire that you land your aircraft at the Bagdad Field immediately."

Farid waved at the Captain.

"This is Mr. Farid Sherazi late of Purdue University. I have my parents aboard....Mr and Mrs Sherazi...who I must get to their home in time for Wheel of Fortune. So I fear that landing here will be impossible."

"Sir, we have orders to fire on you if you do not obey our orders!"

"I see no need in wasting perfectly good....and I might add... expensive missiles in a futile effort to filch my beautiful aircraft."

Farid turned to his computer as the two F- 22s began maneuvering for attack.

"Evade!" he commanded.

As the two fighters converged on their target, it suddenly disappeared.

The two F-22s nearly collided in their confusion. Collecting their senses, they circled the field several times to no avail.

"What the hell happened?" The Captain asked his wingman.

"Beats the shit out of me!" was the answer.

By the time Farid commanded 'cruising speed', the Orion was over the Mediterranean south of Turkey, approximately 5300 miles from New York City, and 5900 miles from home.

Farid turned to his parents sitting behind him.

"How was that for adventure? I'll surely have you home in time for 'Wheel of Fortune'.They both chuckled tentatively, hoping their hearts would hold up for that long.

The Orion sped over Spain, then Portugal, and then over the Atlantic Ocean.

Mars

01/ 05/ '04

"Well done, Farid. I always had confidence in you. Now all you have to do is figure out what you're going to do with the Orion when this is all over."

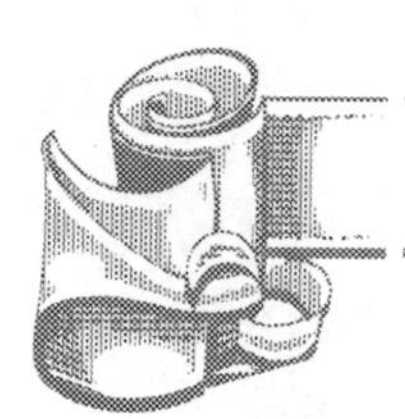

CHAPTER 24

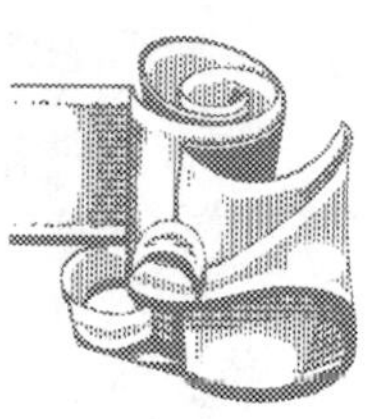

Doc and Crista spent a day touring Amsterdam waiting to catch a military plane back to the States the following day.

Crista appreciated the fact that Doc insisted on separate rooms for their overnight stay.

The following morning, Doc received word that an Air Force C-17 transport was available to them if they could get to the airport in an hour. This was no problem, and before noon, they were high over the Atlantic on their way home

Both the Orion and the C-17 carrying Doc and Crista were headed for New York. It was inevitable that their paths would cross.

The pilot of the C-17 shouted,

"What the hell was that!"

The copilot saw it too and shook his head.

"It had to be going mach 7!"

"Report ahead and see if anyone else saw this thing." the pilot said.

Doc sat by the window on the starboard side of the airplane.

"My God!"

Crista jumped.

"What is it?" she shouted.

"If its what I think it was, you wouldn't believe me,"

The Orion got to New York before the C-17.

As the Orion closed in on the city of New York it slowed to below cruising speed and circled the Statue of Liberty.

"That, Mom and Pop, is what it's all about."

The two of them, sitting on the port side of the aircraft, marveled at what they saw.

"I'm afraid she's something that too many people in this country nowadays take for granted. I'll bet that a large percentage of them don't know that she was a gift from the French people and was dedicated back in 1886, and even what she stands for. When we became citizens we were told that she is a symbol of freedom and democracy to the world."

The words were not cold from Farid's lips when four F-16 jets closed in on them. Orders were to take out the Orion, no questions asked. They converged on the craft from four sides and each fired a missile. The onboard computer registered the danger and reacted on its own. The protective cloak engaged around it and deflected the missiles, and at the same time went into the stealth mode and disappeared from the fighter's screens. Unfortunately, one of the missiles sought out a F-16s and blew it out of the sky. It was all the others could do to escape a similar fate. The Orion was over Pittsburgh before it slowed to cruising speed.

"So much for the Statue of Liberty." Farid said.

Because of the excitement above New York City, all airports were temporarily closed there. Doc and Crista's flight, to their delight, was diverted to Washington D.C.. They debarked from the C-17 and went directly to Walter Reed Hospital and Jon.

"Well, I guess it won't be long before I'll be calling you Mom," he said to Crista after a long hug.

"Whoa!" Doc called out, "Don't rush things, my boy. She may not like the ups and downs of being married to the personnel director of a state park."

Crista hugged Doc's arm.

"I'd marry you no matter what you were." They all grinned.

Jon was able to join the two for lunch in the hospital cafeteria.

"Have they given you any dates for leaving this place?" Doc asked.

"Not since I've been back, but I'm shooting for this May. 'Can't miss the Indy 500." Jon replied lightly.

"What are your plans after you're discharged from the Service?" Crista inquired.

Jon dug into his dish of macaroni and cheese, chewed in thought, and waved his fork toward them.

"I'm thinking of becoming a newspaper writer....maybe a columnist. I'll take advantage of the GI Bill and go to IU, probably, and major in journalism. I think I've got a lot to say to the world."

Doc sipped his water, and responded.

"With that medal, won't they want you to go on tour? You'd be a hell of an inspiration to guys in your condition."

"I won't do it! If I want to inspire, I'll do it on the editorial page."

Crista nodded her head.

"I hate to break this party up, Doc, but our flight is scheduled for departure in an hour."

They left Jon with the hopes that they would be seeing him back home in May.

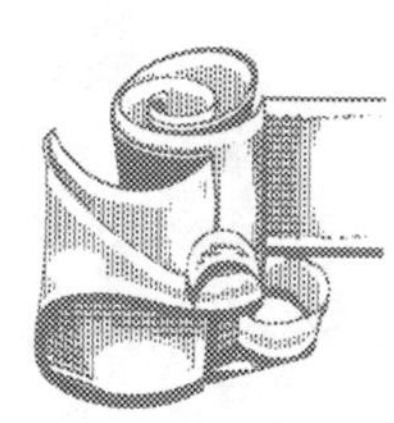

CHAPTER 25

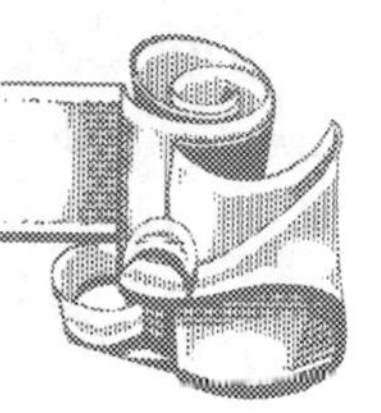

The Orion arrived over the Purdue University airport at 2 p.m.. Farid felt it was unwise to attract the attention of the control tower and surrounding area by landing in broad daylight even in the stealth mode. He had to wait for nightfall. He queried the computer.

"Is this craft space worthy?"

The computer answered back to the effect that it was capable of moon travel, but not deep space. Good enough, he responded. He turned to his parents.

"We've got some time to kill, so we're going on a thrill trip around the world!" He commanded the Orion to "Orbit".

The ship lurched forward and then up into the darkness of space. His parents clutched each other in terror. Surely they would never get to see "Wheel of Fortune"!

Once calmed, they settled back in their seats and looked down on the most breath- taking view of their lives. They were over the Pacific, then Asia, then Russia, and then Western Europe.... All in a matter of minutes.

"Some sight, eh?" Farid bragged, "I could make some money charging tourists for this kind of trip."

It was during the fourth orbit that darkness swept into the midwest with lights blinking on from major cities below. Chicago was the brightest of all, then Detroit. Indianapolis and Cincinnati tied for third with smaller communities dotting the surface of the state.

It was time to land.

Farid ordered the computer to arrange for a taxicab. The Orion, in a stealth mode, put down close to the abandoned hanger at PU's airport. Still invisible to any observer including the Control Tower, it rolled into the hanger. Immediately, Farid jumped from the craft and closed the hanger door.

The Orion, for the time being at least, was secure.

Within minutes a taxi pulled up outside the hanger.

"Time to go home," Farid announced, loaded his parents into the cab, and handed the driver more than enough to get them to their home in West Lafayette.

Thank God, Farid thought as the taxi pulled away. I'm sure they'll enjoy this episode of "Wheel of Fortune."

Mars

01/18/'04

"I ordered the Altair's onboard computer to neutralize the Orion computer. This meant that it would be incapable of any further Altair-like maneuvers. Thus, if taken into custody, it is just a conventional modern aircraft with a sleek fuselage. Sorry, Farid, but that's how it has to be.

Still no word from the Russians. If they are using conventional rocketry, it will be months before they arrive, if they survive the trip. If they're using an advanced system, it would be impossible to predict when they might arrive. In any case, it would be good to see other humans, no matter what their nationality.

Janet is coming along with her pregnancy with little apparent difficulty.The weather outside of the cave seems to have stabilized, so I plan to do a little exploring tomorrow."

Special agents Holtz paid a visit to Robert and Hugo in their dorm two days after the SAD attack on the Tehran airfield.

" I'm afraid our friend Farid is in a little bit of trouble."

Hugo responded, "I heard about the clash with the Air Force over New York City. What charges would be pressed against him?"

"Destruction of government property and manslaughter." Holtz said.

"I just can't believe that he would have fired on the fighters. If his aircraft was a copy of the Altair, it could have just outdistanced them with no problem," Robert retorted.

"True, but nevertheless, he's wanted on those charges, and if you guys know where he is, I'd talk him into giving himself up. It would go a lot easier for him."

Hugo and Robert looked at each other and shrugged.

"Has anyone looked in the abandoned hanger at the airport?" Robert asked.

Holtz chuckled.

"Hell, I don't know. I'm not in the chase. I'm just here to fill you guys in on what the authorities have on this kid."

Holtz rose and walked toward the door.

"They've got an all points bulletin out on him," he said "....local and state police, and CIA agents. You'd be doing him a favor if you persuade him to face up to it." He gave a two fingered salute and left the room.

Hugo walked to the window and waited for the sight of Holtz walking away from the dormitory and down the street. He then turned to Robert.

"Let's go look."

The hanger was empty. There was a note taped to the side door.

All,

I thought you'd go looking for me here. I'll bring everyone up to date. Apparently, the Altair's computer attempted to retrieve all its capabilities from my ship's computer. As they say,...'The Lord giveth, and the Lord taketh away'....but not in this case. Realizing that I was in command of my computer, I ordered it to stand fast,and it did! I am now on my own with the Orion.The Altair is indisposed on Mars, so it now has a back-upon earth. Don't look for me.... you'll never find me.

Farid.

" Oh my God!" Robert blurted.

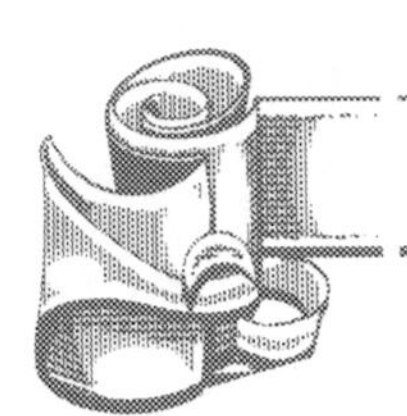

CHAPTER 26

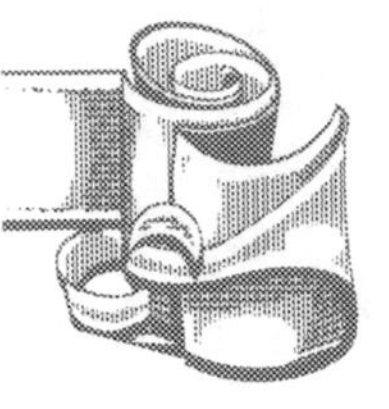

Crista was impressed with Doc's house on a hilltop in Williams Creek. In fact it was so high on the hill she wondered how anyone could get up there on a snowy, icy day. Actually, they couldn't. But fortunately there weren't that many heavy snow days in the winter at the park.

It was a lovely home, surrounded by tall trees, and the essence of the wilderness prevalent in southern Indiana and the Williams Creek area. She settled in quickly, and was amazed that Doc had been enough of a house keeper that there was little straightening up necessary. Maybe adjusting a few picture frames on the wall but that was all.

Until their marriage was consummated, they agreed on separate bedrooms. The date was set for February 21 at the Methodist Church with both a Protestant Minister and a Catholic Priest presiding. As promised earlier when Steve and Becky were married, Steve was to be the best man. Becky was the maid of honor, and Steven, Jr.,was to present the bride.

It was all arranged...with one problem. Steven and Jessica had changed their marriage plans to be on the same date. Steve, at first, was a bit irritated at that, but

Doc had a solution; a double wedding. Robert would be Steven's best man, Jessica's father would present her, and her sorority sisters would provide her wedding entourage of brides maids and a maid of honor.

But who would present Crista? She had a suggestion.... Her brother, Frank, in San Francisco. She had never informed him that she was in the states. Maybe he would be willing to fly here to take part in the wedding.

All applauded the idea, and Crista, hoping that the address and phone number of her brother were still current, called him long distance. His answering machine took the message, and it was later that evening that he returned it. He was excited about the idea, and expressed his gratitude for being asked. It had been years since he had last seen his sister and was looking forward to the trip.

Then it was settled to everyone's satisfaction. The rehearsal would take place on February20. Frank would arrive on February17 and stay with Doc and Crista. He would remain for several days afterwards to become acquainted with his new family, and Crista's new circle of friends.

Mars

02/ 04/'04

"It's impossible to walk around the surface of this planet without wearing protective gear. The main problem is the high amount of ultraviolet rays from the sun because of a thin ozone layer. Plus, the temperature here is extremely low. The protective gear screens out the ultra-violet

rays and keeps temperature at a comfortable 72 degrees.

I tell you this because I journeyed out of the cave this afternoon and browsed around the area. I was alarmed to see what looked like a tornado moving across the horizon, luckily away from my location. The funnel was very narrow, white in color and seemed to reach up into the heavens. The weather on Mars is extremely unpredictable and very violent. I don't think our weathermen on earth would do very well here.

I saw nothing unusual in my roaming, which incidentally, was not too far from the cave.The photos taken by our roamers here show how barren the planet is and that's exactly what I'm seeing. The atmosphere is very thin and is even much less than what it would be on earth's Mt. Everest.The oxygen content on Mars is almost zero and you can't breath without a mask.

As I was returning to the cave, I thought I saw a flash across the sky which I attributed to a meteor.Thus my excursion away from the cave was un-productive. Perhaps if I explore the lake area below it would be more fruitful.

Janet is only days away from delivery.

My computer is acting up again. I'm afraid to inquire as to why."

Farid realized that he was a fugitive after the episode over New York City in spite of the fact that he was not responsible for the loss of an aircraft and pilot. Since he had over-ridden the Altair computer's attempt to negate the Orion's system, he was now forced to make some key decisions. It was frightening to realize that he was in control of one of the most powerful instruments of destruction on earth. He also was aware of the Altair computer's continued effort to override all this. It was a first-time battle of mainframes.

Mars

02/07/'04

"Janet gave birth to Mars Allen Pence at 8:30 a.m. Mars time. He weighs eight pounds, eight ounces, earth measurement.Think of it.... the first true Martian has been born!"

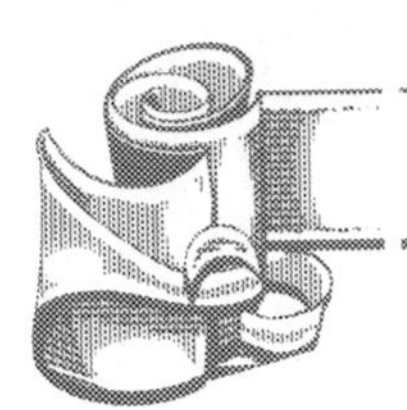

CHAPTER 27

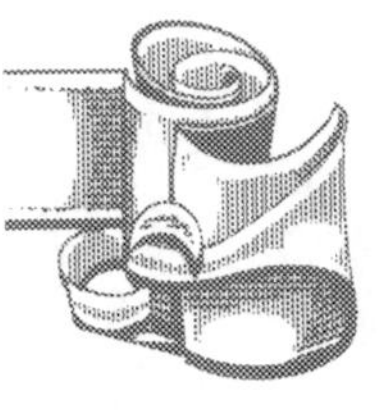

"We haven't seen our son since we returned from that horrid Iran," Farid's father quiveringly responded to the inquiry of several CIA agents at their home.

"Would you have any idea where he might have gone?" was the follow-up question, "Please don't be alarmed, Mr. Sherazi. We mean your son no harm. It seems that all three surviving pilots of the unfortunate engagement over New York City were sure that the missile that struck down the fourth pilot was from one of the clusters fired by them. We just want your son's input."

The elder Sherazi nodded his understanding. He reached for his wife's hand for reassurance.

"Sirs, I thank you telling us that. We have always had faith that our son would never knowingly harm anyone."

"If you hear from him, tell him that he has been cleared of any accusations and to contact us as soon as possible."

They thanked the Sherazis and left.

The Orion and Farid left the hanger the same evening of their return from Iran. He was in control of a machine that could take him any where in the world he wanted to go in an amazingly short time. Under the circumstances, he felt he needed seclusion and time to organize his thoughts, so he had directed his computer to locate and take him to an obscure island somewhere in the South Pacific. It had taken the Orion less than two hours to get there.

Mars
02/16/'04

"Baby Mars and Janet doing well. Pardon my conceit, but I did quite well in the delivery. It could be that the lesser gravity here helped Janet. Just a theory.

The computer informs me that the Orion's computer was able to override my order to neutralize it again. Thus, it looks like we have a competitor on earth. I can only hope that the Farid youngster uses good judgment.

It seems that every hour or so, there was a swishing sound coming from outside the cave. Donning my gear, I ventured out when it was due again. It was what appeared to be a capsule orbiting the planet. I believe it's the Russians. If so, they've made the trip safely and in record time. We'll see how well they do on the landing. Judging from the location of the orbit, I would have to conclude that they know where we are."

Those amazing Russians, Professor Emerson thought. If indeed what the Mars Man saw are the Russians and if they can successfully land on Mars, they have advanced science more than a decade. But what fuel did they use to get there, he asked himself. The known rocket system would eventually get people to Mars, but it would take months, and it's not clear if a crew could psychologically handle the prolonged confinement. No, it would take a new power development to make the trip in as short a time as they apparently did.

One possibility was a fusion rocket. Scientist have been working for over sixty years trying to perfect this process. If the Russians have overcome the main problem with fusion rocketry....the requirement of size and weight, then they have perfected a new source of energy. But the trip, while taking less time, might still be beyond human endurance. The other possibility would be an ion engine. It would require less weight and would result in faster travel. Science fiction movies and novels have used this means of space travel. It could be that the Russians have brought this process into the world of reality.

Doc and Crista stood at the passenger gate at Indianapolis International to greet her brother, Frank Gottlieb. It was not difficult to pick him out. He was six foot three inches tall and extremely trim for a man his age. He excitedly dashed to Crista and hugged her tightly.

He spoke with hardly an accent as he shook Doc's hand with a strong, firm grip.

"You have taken good care of her, Doc. She is as well figured and beautiful as I can ever remember her being."

The trip back to Williams Creek was a delightful exchange of memories between Crista and Frank, with Doc entering an occasional comment.

That evening, notwithstanding Crista's concern that Frank would need a rest after his trip, Doc invited Steve and Becky, Steven, Jr., Jessica and Robert to meet him. He was delighted and showed no sign of fatigue. All were amazed at his friendliness and vitality, and accepted him with open arms. He would make an excellent brother-in-law, Doc thought.

Fortunately for all, both the methodist minister and the priest had had double marriage experience, so the rehearsal on February 20 went without a hitch.

The rehearsal dinner was at the Green Gable Hotel in Williams Creek and afterwards the party adjourned to Steve and Becky's for a nightcap. It was going to be a short night and a long day ahead.

A snow storm came in during the night.

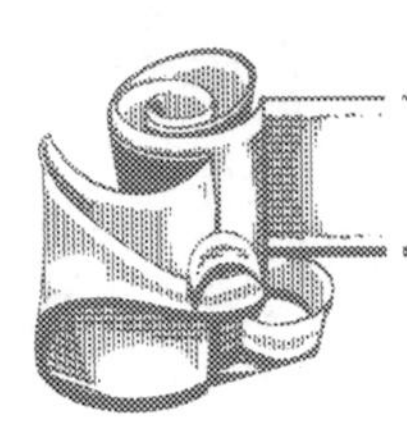

CHAPTER 28

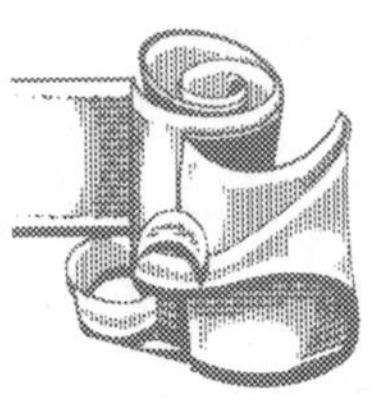

The Orion landed on an uncharted island somewhere in the lower South Pacific. The island was almost a perfect circle with a diameter of roughly six miles. There was an open meadow near the center of the island where the craft set down. Farid moved it into a cluster of palm trees on it's perimeter out of sight from the air.

The sound of surf greeted him as he walked toward the northeast beach area. He stood at waters edge and looked about. There was no apparent human life on the island, but that remained to be seen. Off to the west was the dim outline of another island, perhaps a good thirty miles away.

Farid would have no problem with shelter....the Orion took care of that. Food would be of no concern with the shallow waters teaming with crustaceans, and fish, and the palm trees loaded with coconuts and pineapples.

He felt secure for as long as he remained on the island. He just wished that he felt secure elsewhere.

Now was the time to sit down and think.

The highest point on the island gave Farid a full 360 degree view of the entire island and the surrounding water. It was a good place to do his thinking, he thought, so he hunkered down.

There was five inches of snow on the ground when the wedding parties left for the church. It was still falling when they arrived.

The double wedding proceeded as rehearsed. Crista was the first down the isle on her brother's arm. Doc stood in the front of the sanctuary to the left of the presiding priest, with Steve on his right. Then came Jessica with her father, followed by the maid of honor and the brides maids. Steven and best man, Robert, stood to the right of the aisle in front of their minister. According to standard protocol, the older bride's ceremony went first, followed by the younger.

A sparse audience witnessed the two rites and the final introductions by priest and minister of the two married couples. Jessica and Steven followed Crista and Doc up the isle to the foyer where the wedding parties greeted the small crowd.

One more inch of snow had fallen.

Mars

02/29/'04

"The Russian orbiting stopped yesterday, but I have no idea what's happened to them. If they aattempted a landing I don't know if they were successful or not. I journeyed out of the cave to see what I could see, which was nothing within range. If they set down on top of the mountain housing our cave, I wouldn't have seen them anyway. I wasn't about to try to climb the mountain to check. I figured if they survived, I'd know soon enough."

News flashes all over the world covered the Russian report that the Mars mission had been successful and the crew had landed on the surface safely. The Russians were elated and began a campaign of boasting about the superiority of their space program. There had not, however, been any communications from stations worldwide other than Russia that confirmed the landing. Only the report from the Mars Man seemed to corroborate the Russian claim.

The world waited to hear.

Professor Emerson had moved his astronomy classes to the Goethe Link Observatory in order for his students to be witness to this most extraordinary series of events. He lectured about his thoughts of the significance of it all, and the students gave their opinions. No college curriculum provided by the administration could have offered such an opportunity.

Half the class believed the Russians were telling the truth while the other half thought otherwise.

There were so many questions. Were Gerald Pence and his companion really there? How could they survive without proper food, notwithstanding Pence's statement concerning greenhouse vegetables and edible cockroaches? If true, does Mr. Pence's experience on Mars prove that it's possible to inhabit the planet in the future? What about the baby? If they should ever return to earth, would he be an American citizen, or considered an alien...from another world to boot.

The environment on Mars seems so inhospitable that it was generally agreed by the class that it could never be modified in any way. Therefore, scientists dream of one day populating it was extremely unrealistic.

Eight inches of snow had now fallen in Williams Creek, and it would be impossible to climb the hill to Doc and Crista's house. So they all gathered at Steve and Beckys' . Few outsiders showed up for the reception because of the weather, so most of the food provided for the occasion would wind up in freezers as left-overs. Nevertheless, those in attendance enjoyed the people, the party and the food.

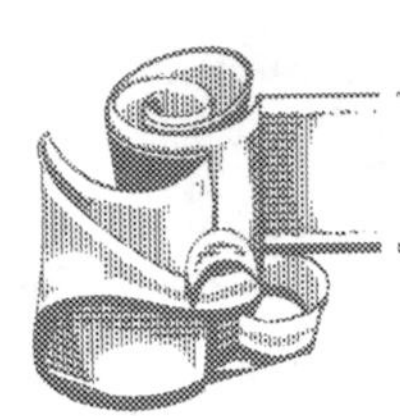

CHAPTER 29

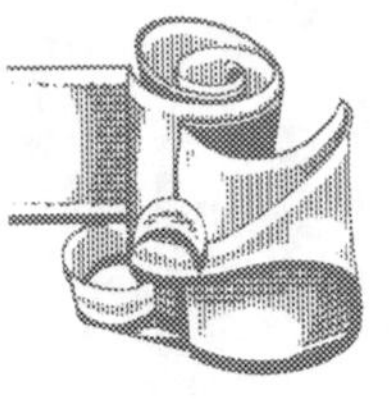

Farid realized that he had to make a decision soon. He could stay on the island indefinitely, but that was out of the question. He could trek around the world living an obscure existence, forever hiding the Orion from the authorities. He could return home and surrender the onboard computer to the wishes of Pence's mainframe, and take his chances with the government. .....or he could fly to Mars!

He chuckled at that thought. Sure...why not? If Pence and the Russians could do it, why not him?

Good God, he thought, am I losing it in the tropical sun?

The thought was ironic, because a driving rain suddenly swept in from the sea and brought his mind back to the hill where he sat. It lasted only minutes, and although it drenched and thankfully gave him a long over due bath, it was a cool rain and invigorating.

The rain stopped and with the sun once again bearing down on him, it got uncomfortably humid. He walked down from the hill toward where the Orion was concealed. He was getting hungry, and if he was going to go fishing, he'd have to fashion some kind of spear.

He walked further into the indigenous forest away from his aircraft searching for a straight, sturdy candidate. The rain had conjured up a dank oder as he traveled deeper into the bush. A howl from a distant creature stopped him.

There was life here after all. Maybe a monkey...a baboon, or a wild dog. These could be dangerous, so the spear he sought would have to be a weapon as well as a utensil. A chirping sound came next. A bird!

It was if the creatures on the island were recovering from the shock of his arrival and were getting back to their normal routines.

He wondered if there were humans here. It was a small island, so he doubted it. But that other island in the distance, was much larger and could possibly harbor a tribe of natives. He could go there and see, but,...no...he'd better stay here for the time being. At least there was no competition where he was.

Dark clouds appeared over the horizon to the East. Another rain...or a storm approaching? He'd better find his spear quickly and get back to the shelter of the Orion. The fishing could wait.

It was a seasonal tropical storm that came to greet him on the island. He sat in the Orion as the wind....maybe 117 miles per hour...rocked it fiercely. The rain spattered the windshield. The sea boiled, and threw huge waves against the shore below. If it got much worse, Farid was determined to leave the island and take the ship above the storm until it subsided. In the meantime, he would lie down and rest. He hadn't realized how exhausted he was. It had been an incredibly involved few days with no sleep and the trap of continuous alertness.

The storm continued and he fell into a deep sleep.

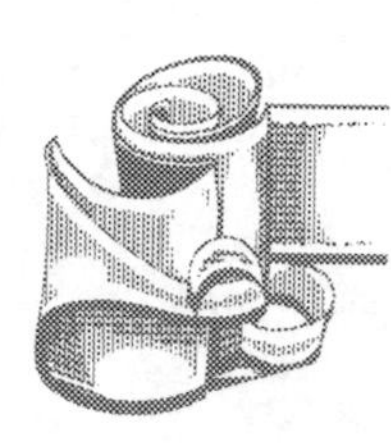

CHAPTER 30

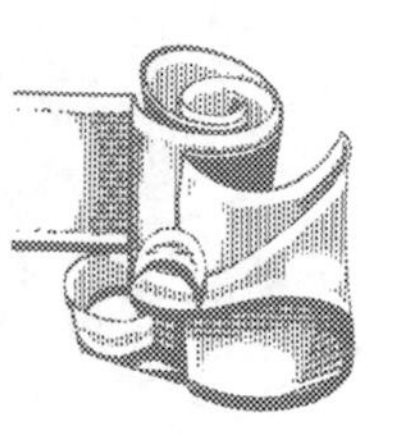

Mars

03/ 03/'04

"It could be my imagination, but I could swear I heard voices this morning. Janet has better ears than I do and she said it was all in my head. Nevertheless, I journeyed out of the cave but found nothing. It's been a day or two since the orbiting had stopped and I had supposed that the Russians had landed. According to transmissions from earth, they claimed they had. Now I was wondering if they had crashed instead.

I decided to suit up and go search the area. Janet argued the point, but I told her we had to determine the fate of the Russians one way or the other.

At first there was nothing unusual. Barren landscape, rock and red dirt was all. Then in the distance I saw what looked to be wreckage strewed about, and further back, a large capsule buried nose first in the ground. Nothing else. No signs of life.

I hurried back to the cave. I convinced Janet that we had to move the Altair out to where the wreckage was, and so we did. I entered the capsule.

Three of the six crew members were dead, their helmets crushed as a result of the impact. Three in the rear were unconscious, but alive. Janet helped me load them into the Altair. The bodies we left for later burial.

We returned to the cave and administered first aid to the three as best we could. Injuries...except for one of them.... seemed to be superficial. The one...a female, later died and we placed the body in the cave outside the aircraft. The other two soon regained consciousness and at first were extremely confused about their whereabouts. The female could speak English, and I tried to convince them they had nothing to fear.

The male was the astronaut, and the female, much to our surprise, was the physician. Her name was Irina Orlovsky.. His name was Ivan Korlov,

She was friendly,..he was not.

He drew a pistol and waved it in our faces, bellowing in athreatening Russian voice. Irina turned to him. "Путь тэ гун дощн ю дан фул. Тэй аре тринг то хелп ус," she shouted. Apparently whatever she said struck home. He lowered the pistol and she took it away from him. So now we have two more mouths to feed. It's getting crowed here.

One thing occurred to me. We may now have the means to journey home if the Russian rocket system is intact on the crashed capsule."

The Williams Creek State Park administration decided that a spring deer hunt was in order. The population had not grown tremendously, but enough so that a preventative shoot was warranted.

"Just like old times," Steve laughed, remembering what they had gone through during the fall hunt of 2000. There were no outside business meetings scheduled in the lodge this spring, so there were no apparent chances of problems this time.

Once again, the local humane association had objected, but as usual it was impossible to get them to understand that it was more humane to lessen the population of deer to save the lives of other park creatures who would suffer the loss of ground food. Also, for the deer themselves, who would eventually eat themselves into starvation.

So the hunters came and left several week-ends later. The kill count was not spectacular, but adequate. Perhaps another hunt was not going to be necessary for a while.

"Some of those guys make me nervous," Doc said to Steve in his office assessing the aftermath of the hunt."All it takes is one idiot to spoil everything. That's why we're so stringent in our screening of the hunters."

"This one was kind of boring," Steve allowed, "but a good boring."

Doc laughed.

"As many problems as you had in 2000, I'd say that boring is good. Anyhow, are things going well with you and Becky?"

Steve nodded enthusiastically,

"Great, and you?"

"All I have to say is I know how to pick 'em! Crista is a fantastic woman in all respects.

I'm sorry as hell for what happened to Jon, but if it hadn't happened I never would have met her. Incidentally, I got a call from him last night."

"How are things going?" Steve asked.

"Super. He says he's hobbling around pretty good now on what he calls his 'fake' leg." Doc grinned.

" I bet he'll make it home before May," Steve ventured.

"I hope so."

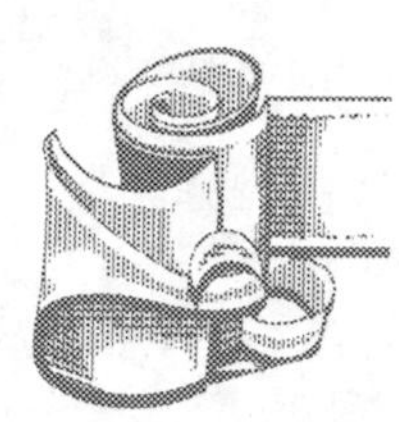

CHAPTER 31

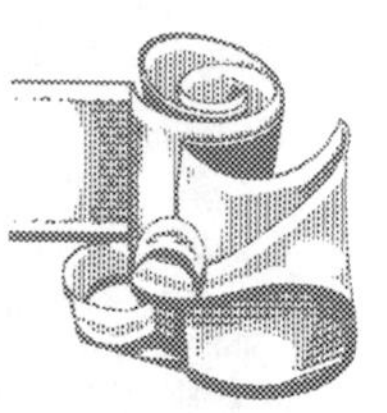

When Farid awoke, the storm had ended. The sun shone brightly and when he left the Orion, the humidity was almost unbearable. He was amazed to see that the northeast beach had been almost completely washed away, and the rest of the island had suffered similar damage.

One more storm like that he thought and the island will be gone. He looked over at the other island and from his vantage point, determined that it had suffered no appreciable harm. He decided to go there.

Robert and Hugo were preparing for finals. They would begin in two weeks, and unless they completely blew the exams, it would lead to graduation for both of them in May.

Agent Holtz had called earlier to find out if either of them had heard from Farid.

"Believe me," Hugo had said, "if and when we do, you will be the first to know about it!" That was that.

It was late in the evening and the boys were studied out. Robert pushed his books aside and turned to Hugo.

"It must be nice to know that you have a job after graduation."

Hugo paused for a moment.

"I never really gave it a thought, but you're right, it beats a stick in the eye." he said,"What're your plans?"

Harold shook his head,

"I'm not sure. I sent resumes to Douglas, and Boeing, but there's been no response."

Hugo leaned forward with his chin on his folded hands.

"I have an idea...but I'm not sure you'll buy it."

"Okay, shoot" Robert offered.

"With your aeronautical background, the Air Force would be for you."

"Air Force!" Robert blipped.

"Yes, the Air Force." Hugo confirmed, "Good money, consistency, and a future of sorts. Hell, with your background, they'd make you an officer right off the bat."

Robert was quiet for a while, and after some thought, he nodded his head.

"I'll think on that one, but it's a hell of an idea."

Mars

04/12/'04

"Ivan had become friendlier, and through Irina's interpretations, had understood my desire to integrate their rocket system with that of the Altair. The engine had survived the crash, and

between Ivan's engineering talents and my knowledge of the Altair, we were able to replace our hydrogen system with the Russian ion engine. We'll be testing it soon.

Irina was quite pleased with Janet's condition after the birth of our son. She was complimentary of my contribution to the delivery which didn't deflate my ego to any extent. Both mother and child are doing fine. Irina is a delight and quite intelligent."

As with the Altair, the Orion's outside surface was painted with a reflective coating which allowed it to become invisible to the human eye on command. It was in that mode when it set down on the second island. This island was almost three times the size of the previous one, and after some brief exploring, it was discovered to be the home of a small tribe of natives.

The Orion was brought back to visibility and camouflaged in a thicket of trees. Apparently none of the natives had seen his arrival, and since the native village was located on the other side of the island, he was able to move about with relative freedom. He was famished, so his first order of business was to find some food. He gathered several coconuts, and with a makeshift spear was able lance several fish. On the beach, away from the sight of human eyes, he built a small fire and cooked the fish. It was extremely boney, so it took him some agonizing time to pick out the flesh before he could eat it. It was chewy and bitter, but anything would have tasted good at this point. He cut open the coconuts, ate the white flesh and drank the milk.

As he sat back, contented, he became aware of being watched. He looked over his shoulder and was shocked to see a native girl staring at him not too far from his camp site. He rose to his feet slowly and stared back at her.

She was lightly colored and slim with long black hair and a round, beautiful face. Her breasts were uncovered, and were small and firm.

He moved toward her, offering a piece of his coconut. It startled her and she ran down the beach. She stopped, turned and started at him again.

"I'm not going to hurt you!" he shouted.

The sound of his voice, echoing down the beach, frightened her and she disappeared into the forest. He tried to follow, but gave in to the tangle of trees and vines. She was gone.

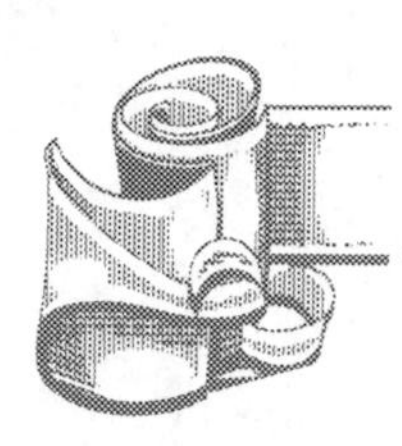

CHAPTER 32

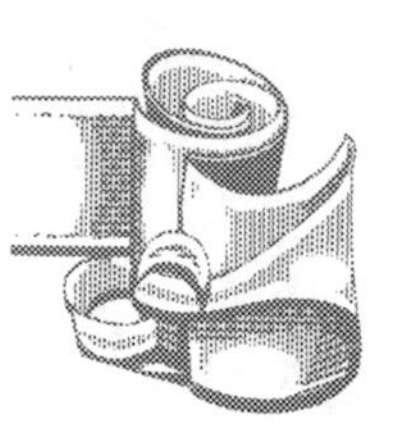

Mars
04/23/'04

"Irina is indeed an amazing person. She is not only a physician, but an artist as well. She's made some incredible sketches of us and the cave we're in. Not having a camera, I was afraid that I could not accurately describe the cave and the lake below...and particularly the mutated cockroaches, that we call, Marsobsters. Now, she is teaching me Russian and Janet is teaching Ivan English.

Russian is not an easy language to learn. Irina tries to make it easier. She points to an object and gives me the Russian name for it: book- Бук ; spoon- спун ; bed- бед, etc.. Irina tells Janet and me that Ivan thinks English is hard to learn also. I've heard it was a very difficult language for foreigners.

Another dust storm has started up, so Ivan and I won't be able to test the Altair and its new rocket system until it's over.

So for now: Год бюэ анд Гос спеед . That's Irina speaking. Get a translator."

The professor turned to his students with a smile. "I understand a little Russian, and what our Doctor Irina has said was: "Good bye and God bless". They all applauded. The Russians were really there.

Robert finished his math class and strolled past the Student Union Building. It was a warm April afternoon and he sat on one of the outside benches to think. What about Hugo's idea of joining the Air Force? It had some merit. Too bad he had elected not to go with the ROTC program here. He would have graduated as an officer, and would have to serve two years of active duty. After that, he could have made up his mind about the future.

Jobs were hard to find these days. He hadn't heard from either Boeing or Douglas, and if he did, they probably would turn him down. He shook his head. Why am I so negative these days? I used to be happy...carefree.

Dad was getting hard to talk to. Granted, he had the right to be. Sometimes I didn't make any sense to him, but his world and mine were on different pages.

The chimes in the Tower began ringing. It brought Robert back to the present.

In any case, graduation was approaching, and it looked as though he had made it with reasonable grades. Not honor roll stuff, but reasonable. He would leave the honor roll to his brother Steven. He got up and proceeded to his next class.

Farid retired to the Orion that night, but couldn't sleep. The sounds of the jungle seeped through to him...the cawing of a bird...the scream of some sort of critter...the pecking of another kind of bird. They were the sounds that he always had heard in South Pacific war movies. Then another sound grabbed his attention...a frog croaking. Where there are frogs there has to be water. He would search for it in the morning.

His thoughts turned to the girl. She was almost Asian looking, so beautiful....so out of place here. He now had two things to look for in the morning. Leaving the island left his mind.

He finally went to sleep.

Steve sat in the avian room in the Nature Center staring out of the one-way window and listening to the birds through the double speaker system. New growth was beginning to form on the surrounding trees, and the bird routine of finding procreation mates gave life to the coming spring.

Things were good now, but there was still the lingering memories of Carolyn. How could it be otherwise? There were many years of happiness with her and the children. Too many to forget.

Becky had understood, as she did all the other eccentricities about him. He felt guilty at times. She had made most of the adjustments in order to make their marriage work. Yes, he thought, he could be selfish and inconsiderate. His guilt centered around the fact that he had fallen in love with Becky even before Carolyn had died.

Was her death his punishment for that? Did she sense it, and did that take away her will to live? Silly, silly, silly thinking, but it was on his mind.

The phone rang in his office across the hall. He got up to answer it.

"Jon's coming home!" Doc's voice boomed, "We're picking him up at the Indianapolis airport tomorrow morning. Would you mind watching the fort?"

"Hell, no! With news like that, I'll even beat off the indians."

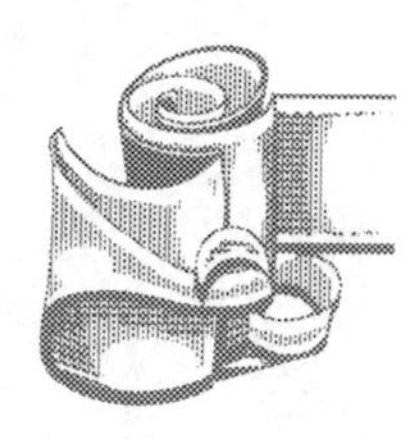

CHAPTER 33

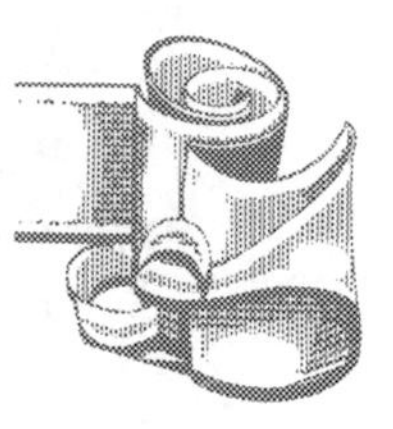

Mars
05/10/'04

"After almost two weeks of dust and wind, the storm here has subsided. After we clean out all the debris in the cave and cave entrance, we'll be ready for our first Altair test run. Keep your fingers crossed.

The media around the world had latched on to the Mars story with vigor. Even the Russians had acknowledged the catastrophic landing of their capsule and the aid given by the Mars Man. The world hung breathlessly on the outcome of the test of the Altair. Columnists speculated the world over what would happen to the spectacular aircraft should it return to earth:

The Washington Post
It is the opinion of this writer that the Altair should be placed in The Smithsonian Institute.

New York Times
By all means, we should have a ticker-tape parade down fifth avenue to honor the Altair and the Mars Man.

Los Angeles Time
The Altair should be destroyed and Mr. Gerald Pence imprisoned for manslaughter (referring to the death of Daryl Atkins in 2002).

Moscow Pravda
The Americans we congratulate on the rescue of the survivors of our Mars mission. We wish to award the American crew with the Moscow Honor Metal and suggest that the air machine be placed in the Air and Space Technology Institute in St. Petersburg.

This whole situation was extremely difficult for Becky. The chance that her father might be returning to earth was a hope that she was afraid to hold on to. The media, by and large, had been cruel, but she understood that that was what they were paid to do.

Steve had to admit that he was wrong in disbelieving where Becky's father was. He felt that he owed it to her to comfort her as much as possible through all this. Still the spring evenings on the patio deck, staring into the starry skies was more of a torture to her than a pleasantry.

"Is he somewhere up there ?" she would ask Steve without really wanting an answer.

Then the message came.

Mars
05/26/'04

"It worked! By God's grace, we are on our way home!"

The professor passed out a list of his student's names and a column for each to predict when the Mars Man would return to earth. The closest to the date would receive an A for the course. All eagerly participated.

Steve's family and Doc, Crista and Jon attended Robert's graduation ceremony on Friday, May 28. He glowed with relief and pride. He shared that with Hugo, who after breaking away from his relatives, was invited to join his family's celebration.

Amidst the hugs and kisses, Robert realized that some time soon he would have to inform his father of a decision he had made, but for now it could wait.

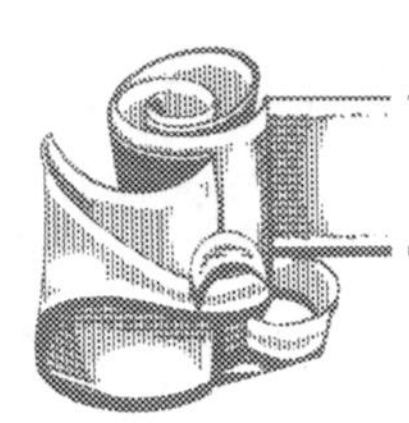

CHAPTER 34

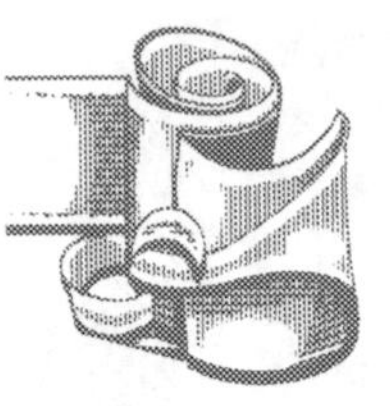

It was a sunny morning on the island and Farid emerged from the Orion fully rested and energized. He was committed to two objectives: to find where the frogs were croaking and the fresh water, and to find the girl. He first set out into the jungle area, picking his way carefully through the tangle of scrubland. A large hawk-like bird grabbed his attention as it circled high over head. That would make one hell of a good dinner he thought.

Suddenly, the bird twisted in the air, and the report of a rifle shot followed. The bird disappeared beyond the jungle area toward the beach on the western part of the island.

He reached the area where he judged the bird to have fallen. There, over the bird's carcass, stood a man, rifle across his arm. He watched as the man grabbed the bird's legs and began dragging it toward the thicket directly in front of him. He suddenly spotted Farid and stopped.

"Who th' ell are you?" he called out with a cockney accent.

He was dressed in soiled khaki shirt and trousers, and wore a frayed Australian bush hat. He was gaunt with a ragged stubbled face, and almost black with constant exposure to the sun. He looked to be in his late fifties.

"My name is Farid Sherazi." he returned.

The man walked closer to him, but left the rifle cradled in his arm.

"To 'ell with your name. 'awed you get here?"

"I flew in!" Farid answered.

The man looked about.

"Flew in, yuh say. There ain't no landin' field 'ere. 'awed you fly in?"

By this time, the man was just a few feet away.

"It's hard to explain. My plane has vertical landing and takeoff capabilities. I don't need a landing field."

The man continued to peruse the area.

"Where is it?" he asked.

"Hidden away! What's your name?" Farid asked.

"Me name is Ben Benson. You see, mate, me ma was a theater person and she was given to stage thoughts, so she gave me 'at name 'cause she felt like it rung like a bell."

"How long have you been on this island?" Farid asked.

"Long enough, mate. Actually, I've lost track o' time. 'Gotta be a couple of years, I suspect."

He took hold of Farid's arm and moved him toward the jungle's edge.

"Yuh look like a reasonable chap. Come join me at my shack and I'll tell yuh all about me, an' yuh tell me about yuhself."

Ben's shack was an incredibly well built tree house, approximately twenty feet off the ground. A rope ladder was the means of getting there and after both had climbed it, Farid was astonished at the interior. Its sides were made of roll-up bamboo slats that could be lifted or dropped, depending on the weather. On one end were several cots, in the center was the living area with bamboo chairs and ottoman. Attached to the ceiling was a fan with a pull rope hanging down that could relieve the sultry days on the island.

"My God!" Farid marveled, " how long did it take to build this?"

"Quite a piece, quite a piece", Ben responded, "but it helped pass the time. 'Ave a seat and let's get tuh know each other. Would yuh care fur a spot of tea?"

"Tea? Yes, I'd love a cup," Farid answered, still amazed at his surroundings.

"Well, it ain't exactly tea." Ben remarked as he moved toward what appeared to be a hot plate, "This 'ere was some of the stuff I salvaged from the ship. I'll tell yuh about that. Th' tea is an herb I found on th' island. Better'n tea, me thinks."

He poured a flask of what looked like pure water into a pan and placed it on the hot plate. He ignited the burner from a canister of bottled gas attached to it.

"Now then," he said returning to his chair, "while that's stewin', let me tell yuh how I got 'ere."

He went on to relate the story of his involvement in arms traffic on islands north of where they now were. They were on a delivery mission. The boat he was on had a crew of four, and half way to their destination they were caught in a violent storm.

"Worse than th' one we 'ad yesterday," he said. "Th' wind blowed us down this way...close tuh this here island and then we capsized."

He went on to explain that the three other crew members apparently drowned, but he was able to swim ashore. When the storm ended, cargo from the boat began washing up on the beach. He pointed toward the hot plate,"That there was one of 'em." He rose and poured boiling water into two tin cups. lifting one of them up,

"These here come up too."

He sprinkled some dried herbs into the cups, and returned.

"Let's let 'em steep fur awhile." He continued his story.

"Among other things, a box washed up that contained some of th.' rifles we was cargoing, along with ammunition.'At was a lucky thing fur me, mate, because it's kept them damn natives away."

Farid perked up, "Natives? What about them?"

"Them bastards ar' mean sons-o-bitches! 'hey tried tuh get me 'ere, but I drove 'em off with 'his 'ere rifle."

" I saw a girl." Farid mentioned.

"Ah yes, Mate, th' girl would be Diesy, I calls 'er. She's like a little cat....shows up and then disappears when yuh try to talk to 'er."

"Does she live in the village?" Farid asked.

" 'Ell no!" Ben returned, " 'at's just it. They 're tryin' to kill 'er."

"Kill her!"

Ben rose, went to the hot plate and returned with the tea. He handed Farid his cup.

"Them natives 'ave a ritual. They gotta sacrifice a woman in the village to th.' gods once a year. It was Diesy's turn, an' she didn't go fur the idea. She run into the jungle and has been runnin' ever since."

" Doesn't she know you'd protect her?"

"She don't trust no one, mate. I've tried tuh get 'er to understand 'at I wasn't gonna 'urt 'er, but she don't understand English, and she jist runs off."

Farid sipped the herb tea and nodded his head.

"Very good indeed." He said, "I noticed that you poured what looked to be fresh water into the pan. Where...?"

"Where did I get it? 'At's an incredible story too, mate. Not far from 'ere there's a pond of clear, cold water. I'll 'ake yuh to it presently. Another thin'. This 'ere island is a regular paradise. In addition to it's pond of th.' most delicious cold water yuh ever tasted, its got all sorts of fruit trees...banana, pineapple, coconut. With all the fish and crabs, yuh ain't gonna starve nohow. Now, mate, what's your story?"

Farid began his story, but in the back of his mind he thought....I can't leave this island with that poor girl in danger..

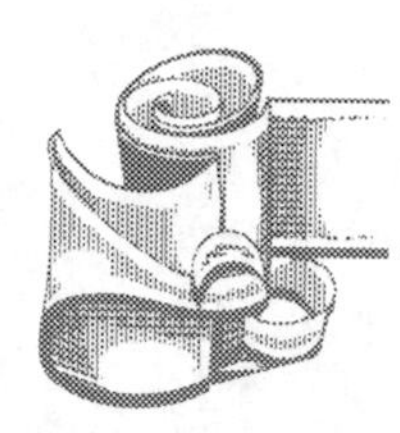

CHAPTER 35

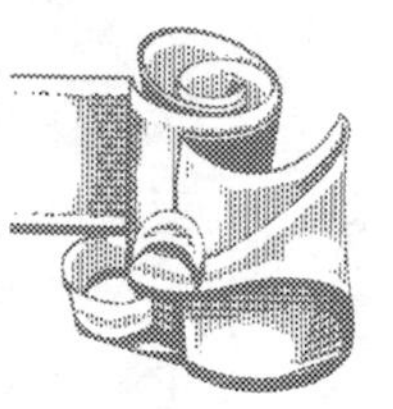

Hugo had left for Washington, D.C. for further FBI training. He soon would be a full-fledged agent. Robert, enlisted in the Air Force the day after graduation. He did this before telling his father because he didn't want to be talked out of it. He told his dad after the fact.To his surprise, Steve had taken the news graciously, as if he almost approved.

"Any particular part of the Air Force?" Steve asked.

"Special Forces" was Robert answered.

Steve cringed,

"That's a tough operation, son."

"I know, Dad. I want it tough."

Robert left for basic training at Lackland Air Force Base in San Antonio, Texas two days later.

May had come and gone. June was half over, and plans for the Fourth of July were in the works for families across the country. There was still no word from the Altair group, and Professor Emerson had moved his class back into the regular class room at the university. All bets on the Altair's arrival date were still on, however. They all waited anxiously.

It was a warm evening. Steve, Becky, Steven and Jessica sat on the back patio sipping their after dinner coffee. The same old owl hooted his presence, and the crickets sang their song loudly...the signature of a summer at nightfall.

Becky linked arms with Steve.

"What are you thinking?" she asked.

Steve thought for a moment and then turned to Steven.

"Tell her, Steve."

Steven wrestled himself to the edge of his chair, and cleared his throat.

"I've had a job offer in Wisconsin as manager of the Blue Mound State Park outside of Madison, and I've accepted." He took Jessica's hand, "In the meantime Jessica will go for her master's at the University of Wisconsin."

Becky rose from her chair and embraced the two of them.

"I hate to see you go, but I'm so proud of the both of you. When do you leave?"

"Next Sunday. I have to be at the Park by the following Wednesday." Steven answered.

"First Robert, now you two." Steve reminisced, "I guess that's what we get for being parents.... an empty nest. Anyway, congratulations!"

Steven and Jessica left for their apartment in Bloomington, and Steve and Becky sat alone on the deck. The moon had risen and its light reflected off of Becky's face. Steve chuckled.

"I'm thinking of that night on Gerald's farm when we stood by the front gate under a full moon, and I told you that moonlight becomes you. You know, for weeks after that I couldn't get that tune out of my mind." He began humming the tune softly.

She smiled warmly.

"How could I forget?"

Mars
5/ 28 '04

"One final word while we're still able to communicate. Before leaving the planet, we took the time to bury the four Russians inside the cave. I suppose if and when the scientists come to Mars, they'll jump to conclusions when they find the remains.

We blasted off in the mid-afternoon, Mars time. We experienced no problems breaking away from the planet's gravitational pull. We instructed the computer of our desired destination, and we were on our way.

It would do no good to try to explain the technical modifications we had to make to the Altair. The ion engine was taken from the surviving equipment of the crashed Russian capsule. Ivan did a remarkable job of improvising all of this.

I won't attempt to explain the ion process, mainly because I don't understand it fully myself. All I know is that it gives us an unlimited source of fuel at incredible speeds.

> *According to our computer, Earth is now approximately sixty-seven million miles from us. Therefore, our estimated time of arrival to Earth at our present speed will be around July 28, barring any unforeseen circumstances.We won't be able to continue our communications until we have achieved the proximity of the side of the moon facing the earth. Until then, au revoir."*

The professor was glad he had continued a vigil at the IU observatory in order to receive what would be the last of the messages from Pence for over a month. He called Dr. Dunbar at Stewart Observatory in Arizona to inform her that he was temporarily shutting down the IU observatory. That done, he turned out the lights and left for the main campus.

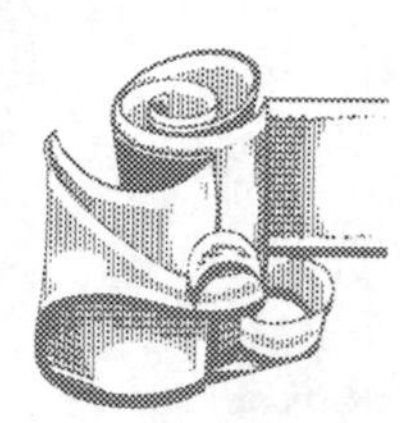

CHAPTER 36

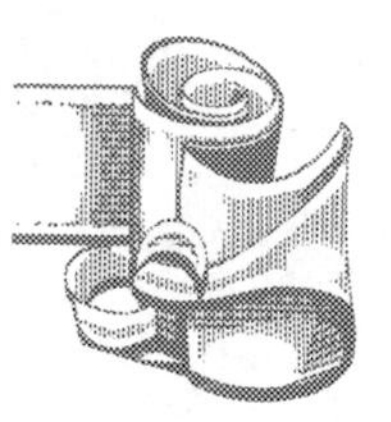

Steve sat down at the kitchen table and read a letter from Robert out loud to Becky:

Dear Becky Mom and Dad,

It's not easy here at Lackland. Forty seven applicants showed up for training, and just fifteen remain...including me. I'm part of the Pararescueman Group for which to qualify you have to make a 500 meter swim, and do it in fifteen minutes or less....I did it in thirteen plus...do six pull-ups in one minute or less...fifty-five seconds for me...fifty sit-ups, forty push-ups, and run the 1.5 mile in 11 minutes,30 seconds or less. I did okay. Most of the candidates failed all of this. I didn't think I was that tough. The training period will be over a year, which will involve stuff you only read about in comic books. As I said, it's tough, but

I love it. I hope I can hang in there.I'll keep you informed of my progress.

Love,
Robert

Steve looked up at Becky.

"Damn, I'm proud of that kid!"

Farid spent the night in Ben's tree house. Aside from the sounds of the jungle he had heard the night before, not much had changed. Sometime during the early hours, however, he heard disturbing rustling below the tree. He rose to his feet and looked down from the deck. He could see nothing. Even the sound had subsided. Probably just the wind, he thought, and he went back to his cot. Suddenly, there was a thump of a spear against the roof of the cottage. It quivered menacingly, as Ben sprang to his feet, yanked the spear from the ceiling, tossed it from his shack, and grabbed his rifle.

"'Ere they go again, them bastards." He crept toward the railing and peered down.Without aiming, he fired a shot into the darkness.

"That ain't gonna kill no one, but it'll scare 'em away fur awhile."

"How can you sleep with those guys creeping around all night?" Farid asked.

" They just tryin' tuh bug me, mate. So far they ain't done me no 'arm, but 'ho knows."

Ben fixed another round of herb tea and they sat on their cots until daybreak.

They ate a breakfast of fruit and nuts. Ben walked to his ammunition box and extracted another rifle and a cartridge bandolier.

"Ere, mate, I want yuh to 'ave this. 'Tween the two of us, I think we kin hold 'em off, if worse comes tuh worse."

"I'm not much of a marksman," Farid admitted.

"Jist the sound does 'em in, mate."

Ben led Farid to the pool of water he spoke of the night before. It was only about twenty feet in diameter, but it was deep, and clear.The bottom was a jade color, and in the very center was a spout that lazily fed the pool with it's contents. There was no doubt that it was uncontaminated.

Ben handed Farid an empty canteen.

"Fill 'er up, Mate. It'll give yuh somethin' tuh sip durin' th.' 'ot day."

Farid helped Ben pluck the fallen bird, and after a proper bathing, they placed it in a pot and onto the hot plate to slowly cook while they toured the island.

"I can't get that young girl out of my mind," Farid confessed.

"Don't be surprised if she don't show up while wer' nosin' around out 'ere. She'll show... then...puff...she's gone, like a deer."

They prowled warily into the thickness of the forest. The creatures there became silent as they progressed deeper. Still no girl...no natives.

Then, in the distance, came the sound of drums beating in rhythm.

"'Em bastards again. Same time each day, they go into their native ritual." Ben observed, " 'at means they'll be looken' fur Diesy again. So be on yur look out fur them and Diesy."

Farid, with Ben following, worked his way to the Orion that he had hidden under trees and brush not far from the tree house.

" I'll be a bloomin' mess, mate. I ain't never seen the likes o' that," Ben uttered in amazement.

" This is where we'll come if we get into trouble," Farid said, "there's nothing those natives have that can touch us here."

Ben reached out and touched the surface of the aircraft.

"This ere's a funny touch tuh it...almost feels alive, it does."

"It's a special skin that can absorb the light and become invisible to the naked eye. It will also repel any kind of ordinance...spears included." Farid quipped.

" 'As it any weapons?" Ben asked.

" It has a laser gun that could blow that native village to kingdom come."

Farid placed his hand on a small LED on the fuselage by the entrance panel. The panel slid open and steps emerged from the bottom. He motioned for Ben to enter.

Inside, there was a control panel with a large flat screen in the center with dials and buttons on either side. The pilot and copilot's seats were in front of the panel, similar to a conventional aircraft. Behind the control compartment were four seats....two on the port side, and two on the starboard side, each with a window. In the rear of the cabin was a rest room facility and a set of cabinets that represented the galley.

Ben let out a long whistle.

" Where th.' bloomin' 'ell did ye get this, mate? Musta cost a fortune!"

Farid laughed.

"You don't know the half of it."

"Ow do yuh start this thing up?" Ben asked.

Farid placed his hand on another LED panel to the left of the pilot's seat.

"This will identify me as the legitimate pilot of the craft. The engines will then start up at my command. I'm thereafter in complete control." Farid indicated the large center screen, "I tell the computer here what I want, and it does it."

"Yuh talks to the bloomin' machine? What's this 'ere world comin' to, mate! I thinks I'm better off livin' in a tree on a deserted island."

Farid motioned to the copilot's seat.

"Would you like a quick ride?"

"Not on yur life! Besides, we'd better be gettin' back to that bird. It outta be done by now."

They left the inside of the plane, covered it back up with brush, and started back to Ben's tree house.

Just as they reached the rope ladder, Ben froze.

"Don't look now, Mate, but Diesy's lookin' at us from that tree behind us. If we pretend not tuh see 'er, we can maybe coax 'er in with a little bit o' the bird."

They nonchalantly climbed the ladder.

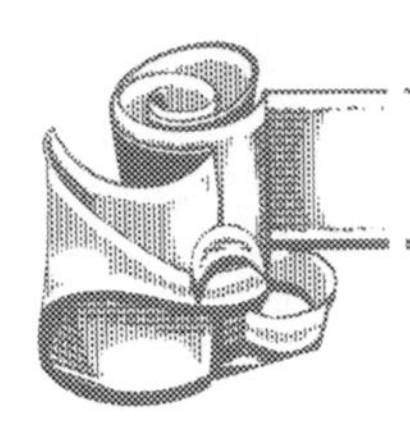

CHAPTER 37

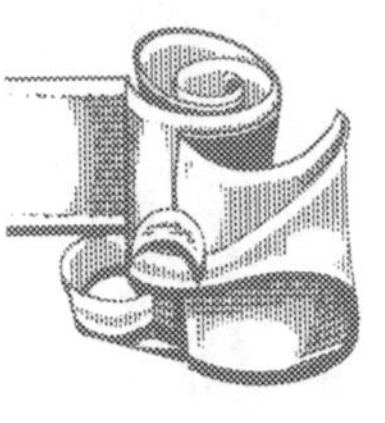

Dear Becky Mom and Dad,

More workouts, and workouts, and more workouts. We've started paramedic training. It's pretty thorough, and when this is all done, I'll probably open up a doctor's office. Ha!

We had hand to hand combat exercises yesterday, I wound up with a shiner, but you should see the other guy.

We'll be going into parachutes next week. It will start with jumping from a twenty-foot tower just to land properly and keep from breaking any bones when the time comes to really jump from an airplane. That will be a thrill.

Two more guys were booted from the program the other day, so now there is only thirteen of us left. I'm still hanging in there so far.

I'll be writing later. Mess call just sounded. At least they're feeding us well.

Love,
Robert

There was illness aboard the Altair. Ivan began breaking out in sores that Irina attributed to his exposure to radiation while working on the engine. Gerald was worried that Ivan's impaired condition would make him unavailable for repairs if anything should happen to the ion system on the Altair.

Another concern was baby Mars's condition. He was running a fever and his skin was turning bluish. Irina was, at first, puzzled. After an extensive examination, however, she came to a strange conclusion. Baby Mars was suffering from his birthplace.

The atmosphere on Mars was obviously different than that of Earth. Baby Mars's system was having problems adapting to the change in the present environment. Both Irina and Janet were in hopes that that would correct itself as they drew closer to earth.

In her spare time, Irina fashioned a set of chess pieces out of a mixture of flower and water baked in the ship's oven. Then came the sixty-four square board and ultimately the games were on. Gerald had not played chess since childhood, and his quick losses to Irina were humiliating

The estimated time of arrival on earth remained July 28.

When Jon arrived home in Williams Creek, and after several days of settling in, Doc and Crista organized a welcome home party for him. Steve, Becky, Steven, Jessica, and all the park staff and maintenance personnel were invited. All but the essential park operating people eagerly attended.

Jon was still adjusting to his prosthetic leg and his cane, although the latter gave him a distinguished air.

He was the hero, but the group appreciated his modesty about it. Over Jon's strenuous objections, Doc insisted that he wear his uniform and his Medal of Honor. He was the warrior come home and everyone loved him.

To Doc's pleasure, Jon mingled with the crowd with Crista beside him, proudly introducing her as his new mother. It was obvious, after time, that he was tiring, so Crista led him to a living room chair where he spent the rest of the evening greeting people.

Jon's weariness was mostly attributed to the fact that he had spent a greater part of the day being interviewed by too many newspaper and magazine reporters and columnists He had been congenial but uncomfortable.

Nevertheless, the party went on until the wee hours of the morning, and the next day didn't begin until after noon.

The following day was all business. His first mission was to obtain his drivers license. He was not happy about it, but in order to qualify, he was given an impaired license and plates. Then Doc accompanied him to Bloomington and the IU campus to register for classes in the College of Journalism. Classes began in early August, so it gave Jon more time to rest and recuperate, although, much to his dismay, the interviews continued. The crowning blow came when his photograph appeared on the cover of one of the Nation's leading military publications.

No rest for the weary, Jon thought.

"Don't look at 'er, mate," Ben said as he began cutting up the roasted bird, "If yuh do, she'll pop right off that tree and....poof...she's gone."

Presently, a portion of bird was attached to a heavy cord and cautiously lowered from the deck facing her tree. She did not move, but eyed the food longingly. It was then that they both saw two natives approaching her tree. Ben grabbed his rifle, ran to the railing and began screaming. Just at that moment, the ground trembled violently. The natives ran in panic.

"Good timing, 'eye, mate? Them shakes is common round 'ere, but now them bastards think I caused it and am some kinda god." he laughed, but the ground shook again... more violently. Ben lost his look of confidence.

"'Gettin' kinda rough! Maybe we oughta get tuh your plane."

The trees began swaying. The girl tried to hang on, but fell to the ground. Apparently uninjured, she disappeared into the thicket as the convulsion grew worse and Ben's tree house began disintegrating.

" Outta 'ere, mate! " Ben screamed, and with his rifle, they both slid down the ladder to the ground below. It was a full blown earthquake in the neighborhood of 8.7 on the Richter scale. They staggered toward the Orion dodging falling limbs and bending against swirling sand.

The quake had uncovered the aircraft and Farid immediately laid his hand on the outside LED. As the hatch slid open, Ben glanced out to sea. The horizon had swelled a good inch and a half.

"My God….a tsunami! It's gotta be a hundred feet 'igh." he screamed above the tumult.

A spear clanked against the fuselage. They turned to face three natives charging them. As Ben attempted to enter the craft, a spear entered his back and he fell backwards onto the ground, driving the spear through his body.

"Them fuckin' bastards got me, mate!" were his last words.

Farid grabbed the rifle and fired blindly toward the natives.To his amazement one of them crumbled to the ground. He turned and barely made it inside. He placed his hand on the control panel LED.

"Let's get the hell out of here!" he screamed as ocean spray began pelting the ship.

The Orion lurched forward and then straight up into the sky.

It climbed above a huge wave that crashed down on the island below. The craft twisted in the swirling air which tried to drag it down into the maelstrom, but the strength of the engines pulled it away an out of danger.

He circled the area. To Farid's astonishment, the island was almost completely submerged. More waves swept below, on their way to other land masses as Farid and the Orion rose out of the earth's atmosphere and into blackness of space.

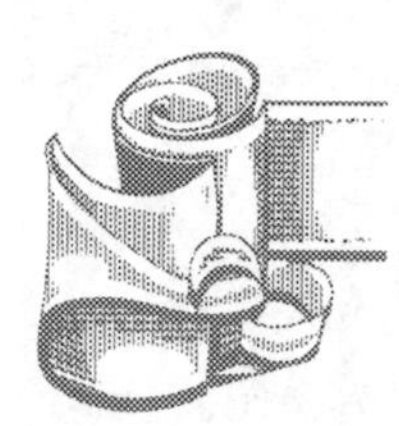

CHAPTER 38

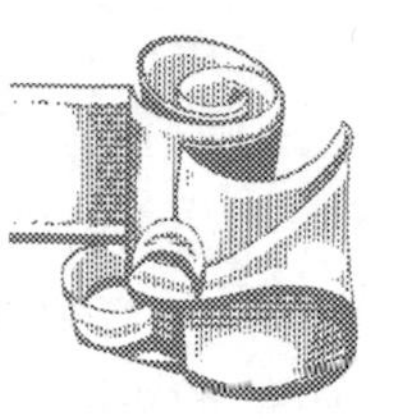

Newspapers, television and radio reported the imagined whereabouts of the Mars Man on his way back to earth. Over and over, the same thoughts came out regarding what should be done when and if he arrived. One late night radio commentator in New York City insisted that the whole thing was a glorified publicity stunt, but failed to say what or who the publicity was for. His program ratings, however, went up remarkably, and to some it would seem that that was what the publicity stunt was all about. Each evening he had a different scenario to back up his claim, and people listened because it was good entertainment if nothing else.

As long as the world wasn't coming to a end, there was nothing more important to report than the status of the Mars Man.

Once again, throughout all of this, Becky was standing fast, because she had her family's love and support. What ever happened, would happen no matter what.

Ivan was getting worse. The medicine that Irina was giving him was having less and less effect, and soon he slipped into a coma. If anything happened to the mechanics of the Altair now, all was lost. Baby Mars appeared to be stabilizing, and to both Irina and Janet's relief, he seemed to be regaining his normal coloring.

They were approaching the back part of the moon, and based on that fact, their ETA time would be earlier than expected. The media didn't anticipate that.

Gerald achieved a draw on his most recent chess game with Irina. He was catching on, even tough his queen's head came off during the final move. Gerald jokingly accused Irina of poor craftsmanship. Janet watched the games with deep interest and finally challenged Gerald to a game when she felt confident enough. She was a natural. The fact that she beat him in twenty moves was the crowning humiliation. He threatened to quit the game of chess completely.

Earth's moon loomed before them and Irina noted some signs of improvement in Ivan's condition.

Jessica missed her period much to the excitement and expectations of all. She was due to see her physician the following week, but she was pretty sure. Father-in-law Steve made the comment that before long they would either have to add on to the house, or look for a larger one when the kids came visiting...all in fun of course. The news stimulated the shopping desires of both Becky and Crista. Together they did the shopping in downtown Williams Creek not knowing as yet what gender the baby would be. It was just fun doing it, and doing it together. The big items such as a crib and bassinet, and rattles and such, were easy decisions, but clothes were guesses that they purchased with the understanding that they could be returned gender pending.

On the day of July 16, the word came to both of them that Jessica was indeed expecting. Due date: late March, 2005

Dear Becky Mom and Dad,

My bunk mate broke his ankle on a jump from the parachute training tower two days ago and I'm afraid he's out of the running. We're down to ten guys now since one more was bounced last week. I'm getting a little nervous about things. I never thought I was that good at anything. So far, though, I'm coming along. Wish me luck.

Love, Robert

Steve sat down and wrote a return note to Robert.

Dear Son,

Becky and I are always glad to hear from you and that you're doing so well in your training. You mentioned in your last letter that you didn't think you were that good at anything. Well, your mother and I think you are.

Many years ago, when I was down on myself like you seem to be, my grandfather....your great grandfather.... told me to remember my heritage. There are many generations of Gordons that are standing behind you and pulling for your success. You can't see them, but they are there. You mustn't let them down. Be a Gordon! Hang in there like we know you can and will..

Your brother will be a father come March of next year. Another Gordon to be proud of. God bless you, Son.

Our love,
Mom and Dad

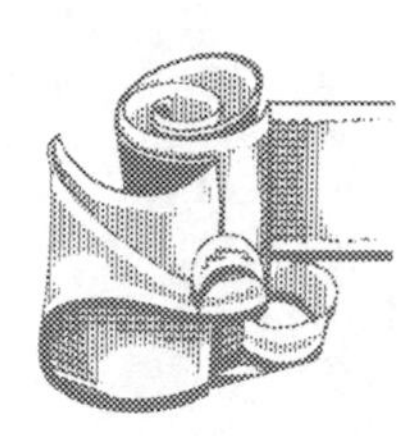

CHAPTER 39

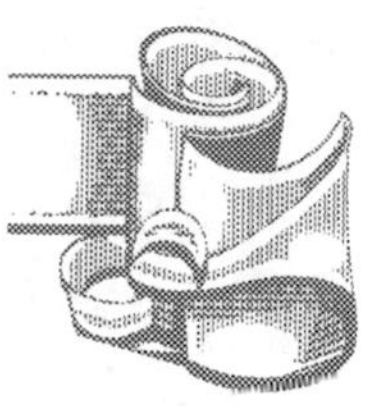

Farid was exhausted. He sat almost trancelike in the pilot's seat and tried to think. Ben and the native girl were gone. Very little appeared to be left of the island....perhaps the smaller one too. Now the question was...were to go and when.

The Orion drifted over the Asian continent. He dozed momentarily, and as they sailed over Western Europe, the onboard computer startled him awake.

"I am receiving a message from the Altair. It appears to be in the vicinity of Earth's moon. It is returning from Mars. How shall we respond?"

Gerald was just as startled when the main computer aboard the Altair sprang to life.

" This is a message from the Orion. We are not hostile. We henceforth will obey all commands from the Altair. What instructions do you have?"

Gerald sat back in his seat and thought. To his computer:

"Tell The Orion that we will be arriving on Earth tomorrow night. We will set down in the stealth mode in the field adjacent to the Williams Creek State Park Administration Building. We will then debark all personnel and with the assistance of the Park Staff will determine our course of action thereafter."

"Message received and will concur!"

With time to kill, Farid leaned back and went to sleep.

The worldwide news service was suddenly in an uproar. July 28 was approaching and Mars Man had not announced his pending arrival .He seemed to have vanished into thin air. Newspapers, radio and television stations in numerous countries and in numerous languages reported in sheer panic:

Mars Man Disappears
There have been no reports from any astronomical stations throughout the world of contact with Gerald Pence aka The Mars Man or his machine.

The late night radio commentator in New York City asserted that it validated his claims that it had been nothing more than a clever publicity stunt. He began suggesting beneficiaries such as cereal...Mars Man Flakes, or a candy bar...Mars Man Bar, or underclothes....Mars Man Skivvies etc.. He was in his glory...for a while. The missing recipient of all of this would be headline news as long as the suspense was there. When that began to wane, so did our late night host's ratings. As time went on, he would be just another boring late night radio host.

There was no moon on July 26 so when the Altair landed in the stealth mode, there was no chance of an inadvertent sighting. It settled quietly on the Park field followed shortly by the Orion. Doc and Steve had been alerted of their arrival and stood by the rail fence watching their descent.

Gerald emerged from the Altair followed by Janet with the baby and Irina. According to their advanced instructions, a gurney had been provided by the IU hospital for the comatose Ivan. Farid stepped down from the Orion.

The group huddled.

Doc informed Irina that he would call for a helicopter to transport Ivan to the hospital after the two aircraft vacated the park field.

"What will we do with those?" Farid asked Gerald, waving toward the aircraft.

"Send them where they will never be found." Gerald responded. With that he spoke softly into his cell phone, and within seconds both craft lifted off the ground, and quickly disappeared into the night.

"Where is this place they will never be found?" Farid persisted.

Gerald pocketed his phone.

"Let's just say that the less is known, the less is the worry."

Farid did not care for the answer, but he realized that that was all Gerald was going to say on the subject.

Doc called for the helicopter and upon its arrival they loaded Ivan aboard. Irina approached Gerald beneath the whirling blades.

"I will accompany him and give the medical team my report on what I know of his condition. If you're curious, I do not intend to return to Russia, but I'll talk to you about that later."

She climbed into the helicopter and blew everyone a friendly kiss. It lifted off and disappeared over the trees.

The field gave way to the sounds of a late summer night, and the group silently convened in the Administration Building. Coffee was waiting and they sat down around Doc's desk to discuss future plans.

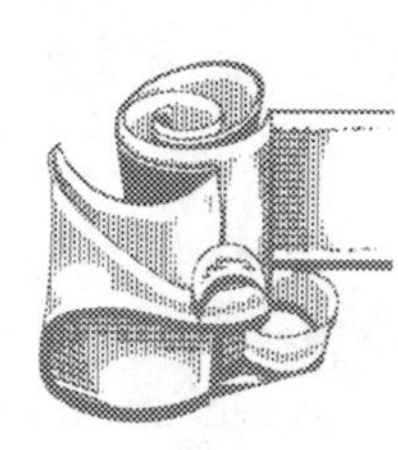

CHAPTER 40

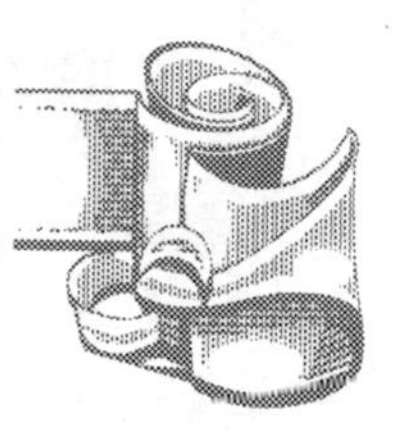

Dear Becky Mom & Dad,

Here it is November already. I've been here for six months and counting. We're now down to eight guys, and judging from the caliber of them, its probably going to stay that way. Incidentally, I don't think I told you how *much I appreciated that terrific letter you sent me awhile back. It sure gave me a lift. It's probably responsible for me still being here.*

We've had several jumps since my last letter. I was scared at first, but it's gotten to be fun. In a couple of weeks, I'm told that we start the free fall phase. That's where they bail us out at twenty-thousand feet and we fall until the ants below look like people and then we engage our chutes. That might be a little..er... antsy. Don't worry. If my chute doesn't open, I'll take it back for a new one. Ha,ha.

My love,
Robert

As a result of the meeting in Doc's office, Farid was given the position of Electrical Maintenance Supervisor at Camp Drew, a military reservation north of the Williams Creek State Park. His mother and father were assigned as house maintenance personnel at the park lodge and given a small cabin on the grounds as their home. In order to avoid the chance of being recognized, Gerald and Janet were also assigned positions at Camp Drew out of the path of tourist traffic. They also became Mr. and Mrs Philip Jackson, and Gerald fulfilled a life long wish by growing a full beard. The baby's name was changed to Marion P. Jackson.

The Russians objected strenuously to Irina's desire for diplomatic asylum and accused the United States of kidnapping her. Nevertheless, she was granted her wish and shortly afterwards applied for US citizenship. She obtained a job with the Department of Veterans Affairs as a doctor at the VA hospital in Indianapolis.

Ivan did not survive his radiation poisoning and the Russians blamed the United States for improper medical treatment. Tensions between the two nations whirled back and forth until it ran its course weeks later.

There was another startling event. Through some incredible miracle, the native girl,(Daisy), survived the tsunami that washed over her island, and was rescued by a New Zealand helicopter. She was taken back to New Zealand for recuperation and an introduction to the civilized world.

Dear Becky Mom and Dad,

I've reached the final stage of my Special Forces training and this will be the toughest part. They're hauling me up in the wilderness of the State of Washington and setting me free to roam on my own for four weeks.

They give you a rucksack, a knife, flint, a small a amount of food, and a poncho liner. With just these few items you are expected to find food and shelter, and protect yourself from the beasts of nature. That'll be no. easy task, since there are bears and wolves all over the place.

If you don't hear from me, don't eat any bear meat. I might be a part of it. Ha!

Love,
Robert

P.S. I got a nice letter from Jon Ewing. He's not out of school yet and already he's been hired as a columnist for the military magazine whose cover he was on some time ago. Aren't we one happy family?

The final disappearance of the Mars Man made good media bait until a tragic explosion in a mall in the city of Peoria killed 43 people. So much for the world's concern about Mars Man.....and where did Gerald send the Altair and the Orion?

Jessica gave birth to twins and in celebration, Steve and Becky sat on their patio deck that evening, wine in hand. They tapped glasses... and couldn't have cared less where the two super crafts had gone to.

"Here's to Robert, Steven, Jessica... and the twins."

#

POSTSCRIPT

Gerald and Janet were officially married in the chapel at The Drew Military Reserve. Steve and Becky were witnesses with Steven and Jessica also in attendance. During this ceremony their names were changed, and Marion P. Jackson, aka Baby Mars, was baptized. The two of them enjoyed the rest of their lives free of tension and anxiety. Gerald died in 2032. Marion, with his mother as agent and coach, became state chess champion and was declared the youngest player to do so. His chess future was bright.

Steve Gordon lived to see his family grow in size until the year 2041 when he passed away peacefully knowing that he had done his best in life. **Becky** stayed in their cottage and entertained her family at every opportunity. She followed Steve in death in 2052.

Doc and Crista retired to the sunshine of the Florida coast Doc died of a heart attack in 2024. Crista then moved to California to live the rest of her life with her brother. She never re-married.

Steven became regional manager of four state parks in Wisconsin, Illinois, Iowa, and Ohio. **Jessica** became a professor of biology at the University of Minnesota, in addition to giving birth to one more child.

Robert passed the special forces training and spent 30 years in the military. He retired at the age of 51 a

Full-Colonel. He married during his service time, his wife producing two healthy children.

Jon became the editor-in-chief of the military magazine that originally hired him after he graduated from IU. He also was renowned for his writing talents and wrote many articles for leading publications the world over. He was author of four non-fiction books.

Irina became an American citizen in 2009, and after many hassles, was able to bring her mother to the United States. She was highly successful in the medical field. In spite of several proposals, she never married.

Farid spent an uneventful career at the military reservation until, while on vacation, the aircraft he was aboard disappeared over the Pacific in 2018. He never knew that his native girl **Daisy** was still alive.She ultimately married a doctor in Wellington, New Zealand, and had three children by him.

Hugo became a district FBI Special Agent, and would be involved part time in the protection of the President of The United States. He would never marry. He and Robert corresponded with each other for the rest of their lives.

And to the reader–Where did the Altair and Orion go?

Any where you want them to!